# MATHEMATICS
## IN
# RELIGION

**Rajesh Kumar Thakur** currently works as the Honorary Director at the National Vedic Maths Academy, a branch of the All India Ramanujan Maths Club (AIRMC), Gujarat, and is the Chairman of the Award Selection Committee of AIRMC. He is a postgraduate in three diverse subjects— Mathematics, Operational Research and Education—and is a Doctorate in Education on Vedic Mathematics.

Rajesh has been teaching secondary and senior secondary school students for the past fourteen years and has written more than 30 books and around 150 mathematics articles and dozens of research papers in national and international journals. He has conducted several talks and national-level quiz shows on the All India Radio and in National Mathematics Convention. He loves writing poems, dozens of which have been published in various magazines of repute.

Rajesh has received many awards, including the National Best Teacher Award by AlRMC in 2010, Appreciation Award (2012) and Mathematica Accolade of Honour (2014) by International Young Mathematicians' Convention (IYMC). In 2014, the AIRMC honoured him with a Special Achievement Award for conducting 125 free workshops on mathematics in the year 2012. He has also received the Lalit Kishore Pandey Yuva Lekhan Award 2015.

Also by the author

*The Essentials of Vedic Mathematics*

*Maths Made Easy*

# MATHEMATICS
## IN
# RELIGION

RAJESH KUMAR THAKUR

RUPA

Published by
Rupa Publications India Pvt. Ltd 2016
7/16, Ansari Road, Daryaganj
New Delhi 110002

*Sales centres:*

Allahabad Bengaluru Chennai
Hyderabad Jaipur Kathmandu
Kolkata Mumbai

ISBN: 978-81-291-4203-0

First impression 2016

10 9 8 7 6 5 4 3 2 1

The moral right of the author has been asserted.

Printed at Nutech Print Services, Faridabad

*To*
*My Sweet Daughter*
*Nishtha Thakur*

# CONTENTS

# PREFACE

यथा शिखा मयूराणा, नागानां मणयो यथा
तद् वेदांगशास्त्राणा, गणितं मूर्धनि वर्तते

Like the crowning crest of a peacock and the shining gem in the cobra's hood, mathematics is the supreme Vedanga Sastra.

The contribution of Vedic literature in the field of mathematics is immense. The number 0 is the gift of the Hindus of antiquity to mankind. The concept itself was one of the most significant inventions in the history of mathematics. The place-value system, big numbers, decimal system, the concept of infinity and the geometrical concept of constructing altars in different two-dimensional shapes taught the world the very principle of Pythagoras theorem much before Pythagoras was born. The Vedas, Puranas, Upanishads, Ramayana, Mahabharata, and other religious texts of ancient times not only demonstrate the fabulous knowledge of Vedic scholars but also build a strong foundation of different mathematical concepts.

No doubt the concepts of Pascal Triangle, Fibonacci sequence, Taylor series, Permutation and Combination, Trigonometry, Binomial Theorem, etc., were known to Indians even before Western mathematicians started working on it.

My book is based on research conducted over four years. I want readers, especially young ones, to understand that the root of mathematics lies in religious texts and that it is important to study them and discover the mathematical concepts hidden in them.

I am sure that I have not done enough justice with my research. I should have devoted about fourteen years, not just four, to study this topic. I do, however, believe that this book will get more young people to do research in this field. The government should work towards promoting this idea.

I would like to highlight that the purpose of this book is to showcase mathematical concepts hidden in the religious texts, and not to favour or hurt any religious sentiments.

I could have added a few more chapters on trigonometry and astronomy but decided to focus on them in the revised edition later based on the feedback of the readers.

I am thankful to my wife who was the constant support in writing the book; Anita Sharma, Principal of S.D. Public School, Pitampura; Chandramauli Joshi, Chairman of All India Ramanujan Maths Club, my parents, Vidya Patil (maths teacher at Sanskardeep Vidhyalaya, Ankleshwar in Gujarat); Rashmi Kathuria (PGT at Kulachi Hansraj Model School, Ashok Vihar in Delhi) for their support. I am also thankful to Virendra Kumar (rtd lecturer from Aligarh) who guided me while writing this book.

I would also extend my sincere thanks to the authors whose names and work have been acknoweldged in the book. I have taken the help of more than 100 research papers, religious books of different religions and websites like Hindupedia and Wikipedia to gather information about this book.

I find myself privileged that R.K. Mehra of Rupa Publications has shown faith in me. I am extremely grateful to him for giving me the opportunity to learn about different religions in context of mathematics.

I do hope readers will encourage me by sending their valuable suggestions and feedback.

**Dr Rajesh Kumar Thakur**
Mail Id: rkthakur1974@gmail.com
Twitter handle: @R_K_Thakur

# 1

# MATHEMATICS IN RELIGIOUS TEXTS

Mathematics is omnipresent—be it in business, architecture, designing, engineering, war, nature, universe, or religious texts. C.F. Gauss rightly said, 'God does arithmetic.' Isaac Newton was also right when he said, 'God created everything by number, weight and measure.'

Number has become our true friend since the time we started thinking about the need to use it in our daily lives.

Religious texts are full of mathematics. Since mathematics has no religion and it is for the service of humankind, I have studied the mathematics in different religions particularly focusing on numbers.

## Hindu Religion

According to the Supreme Court of India—unlike other religions in the world, the Hinduism does not claim any prophet, it does not worship any one god, it does not believe in any one philosophical concept, it does not follow any one religious rite or performance; in fact, it does not satisfy the traditional features of a religion. It is a way of life and nothing more. There is no specific holy book that is supreme in Hindu religion. The Vedas, Upanishads, Puranas, Upavedas, Vedangas, Ramayana, Mahabharata, etc., are the sacred texts of the Hindus. The sacred texts of Hinduism fall under two cateogries—Shruti (heard) or Smruti (remembered). Shruti scriptures are considered pious, divinely inspired and authoritative texts for belief and practice, while Smruti scriptures are the thoughts of rishis. The Vedas could be called the supreme religious text of Hinduism. So let's begin our journey of unearthing mathematical knowledge from the Vedas.

## The Holy Vedas

The Vedas have guided Indian civilization for thousands of years. The four Vedas (explained later) are the pillars of Hinduism. Manusmriti calls them the source of all dharmas. There is no major religion on the planet, which has not been influence by them. The best definition of the Vedas according to me is the one given by Sri Sankaracharya Bharti Krishna Tirthaji Maharaj who is attributed to being the father of Vedic Mathematics. According to him, the very word Veda has a derivational meaning—the fountainhead and illimitable storehouse of all knowledge. This derivation, in effect, means that the Vedas contain within themselves all knowledge needed by mankind relating not only to the so-called *spiritual* matters, but also to those usually described as purely secular, temporal or worldly.

*An eighteenth-century manuscript of the Rig Veda.*
*(Source: http://www.nandanmenon.com/Rig Veda.htm)*

There are four Vedas: a) the Rig Veda b) the Yajur Veda c) the Sama Veda and d) the Atharva Veda. Each is further classified into four major texts—Samhitas (text on mantras and benedictions), the Aranyakas (text on rituals, ceremonies, sacrifices and symbolic sacrifices), the Brahmanas (commentaries on rituals, ceremonies and sacrifices) and the Upanishads (text discussing meditation, philosophy and spiritual knowledge).

According to Muktikopanishad, the Rig Veda had 21, the Yajur Veda had 109, the Sama Veda had 1000 and the Atharva Veda had 50 branches with over 100,000 verses. Though we can only find around 20,379 verses in total from all these Vedas. The Rig Veda contains 10522 verses or 1017 hymns arranged in 10 books called mandalas; the Yajur Veda contains 1975 verse-mantras in 40 chapters; the Sama Veda contains 1549 verses; and the Atharva Veda contains 5977 verses in 20 chapters.

Renowned physicst Stephan Hawkings says,

'Vedas might have a theory superior to Einstein's law $E=mc^2$. The Satapatha Brahmana 7-1-2-23 and Gayatri Mantra talk about Universe being threefold (triloka): Prithvi (Earth), Antariksha (the space in between) and Dayu (Heaven).

'McCauley's Educational Act of India (dated Feb 2nd 1854); aims at transforming Indians to be English in taste, morals and opinion. I strongly feel the process of westernization has brought about a psychological slavery among Indians who'd opt to be Engineers rather than Vedic scholars, given a choice.'

Vedas are a vast storehouse of knowledge, abundant information and solutions waiting to be discovered by dedicated youngsters.

The famous Danish physicist and Nobel Prize winner Niels Bohr was a great follower of the Vedas. He said, 'I go to the Upanishads to ask questions.'

The Rig Veda is also called the Veda of Praise as it contains hymns of praise to various gods such as Indra and Agni. The Yajur Veda is also known as the Veda of Rituals as it contains hymns recited by priests to perform sacred rituals. The Sama Veda is known as Veda of Melodies as it contains songs used during various occasions. Finally the Atharva Veda is also called the Veda of Chants and contains prayers, spells and incantations.

The great Indian philosopher Sri Aurobindo expressed the following view about the Vedas: 'I seek a light that shall be new, yet old, the oldest indeed of all lights...I seek not science, not religion, not Theosophy but Veda—the truth about Brahman, not only about His essentiality, but about His manifestation, not a lamp on the way to the forest, but a light and a guide to joy and action in the world, the truth which is beyond opinion, the knowledge which all thought strives after—yasmin vijnate sarvam vigna—tam (which being known, all is known); I believe it to be the concealed divinity within Hinduism...I believe the Veda to be the foundation head of the Sanatan Dharma; I believe it to be the concealed divinity within Hinduism,—but a veil has to be drawn aside, a curtain has to be lifted. I believe it to be knowable and discoverable. I believe the future of India and the world to depend on its discovery and on its application, not, to the renunciation of life, but to life in the world and among men. I believe the Vedas to hold a sense which neither mediaeval Indian nor modern Europe has grasped, but which was perfectly plain to the early Vedantic thinkers.'

In the Vedas, there are instances which show that people at the time were also using ten fingers to count. In a mantra in the Rig Veda, the words awani, kaksya, yoktra, yojana, etc., have been used to count with the help of finger.

दशावनिभ्यो दशकक्ष्येभ्यो दशयोक्त्रेभ्यो दशयोजनेभ्यः।
दशाभीशुभ्यो अर्चताजरेभ्यो दश धुरो दश युक्ता वहद्भ्यः॥

ऋग्वेद 10. 94. 7

There are instances in Vedas where numbers from 1 to 9 are used and 9 is considered the largest among the one digit numbers. The names for the numbers 1 to 9 are—eka (1), dve (2), tri (3), chatur (4), pancha (5), shat (6), sapta (7), asta (8) and nava (9).

The Vedas speak about various numbers that are big in size. Surprisingly, it talks about the number 0 and infinite. The Vedas speak about 33 gods that Hindus should worship and they are 8 Vasus, 11 Rudras, 12 Adityas along with Indra and Prajapti.

In the Vedas, number are mostly in multiple of 10 except the cases of certain number like 34.

In an article published in *The Hindu* on 19 February 2002 by N.S. Rajaram, the usage of the number 34 in the Vedas has been discussed. In verse 1.162.18, the Rig Veda describes a horse having 34 ribs (17 pairs). Fossils remains of Siwalik horse show the presence of a 34-ribbed horse in India going back tens of thousands of years.

In Krishna-Yajur Veda, there is reference to numbers in decimal system:

सकृत्ते अग्ने नमः। द्विस्ते नमः। त्रिस्ते नमः। ...............
दशकृत्वस्ते नमः। शतकृत्वस्ते नमः। आसहस्रकृत्वस्ते नमः।
अपरिमितकृत्वस्ते नमः।

(O fire, salutation unto you once, salutation twice and salutation thrice…

Salutation 10 times, salutation 100 times, salutation 1,000 times and salutation unto you infinite times.)

न द्वितियो न तृतीयो चतुर्थो नाप्युचते।
न पंचमो न षष्ठो सप्तमो नाप्युच्यते।
नाष्ठमो न नवमो दशमो नाप्युच्यते।
तामिदं निगतं सहः स एष एक एव वृदेक एव ।
सर्वे अस्मिन् देवा एकवृतो भवन्ति।
(अथर्ववेद कां0 13 अनु0 4 मंव 16–18, 20, 21)

This mantra tells that God is one. There is no 2nd, 3rd and 4th god in the universe. There is no 5th, 6th and 7th god. Not even 8th, 9th and 10th god is present. He is the supreme one and unique and there is none other god in the universe.

The formation of numbers is also evident from the Richas (shlokas) of the Vedas. In Taitriya Samhita of Yajur Veda, the following shloka describes beautifully the formation of odd numbers:

एका च मे तिस्रश्च मे, तिस्रश्च मे पंच च मे,
पंच च मे सप्त च मे, सप्त च मे नव च मे,
नव च मे एकादश च मे, एकादश च मे त्रयोदश च मे,
त्रयोदश च मे पंचदश च मे, पंचदश च मे सप्तदश च मे,
सप्तदश च मे नवदश च मे, नवदश च मे एकविंशतिश्च मे
एकविंशतिश्च मे त्रयोविंशतिश्च मे, त्रयोविंशतिश्च मे पंचविंशतिश्च मे,
पंचविंशतिश्च मे, सप्तविंशतिश्च मे, सप्तविंशतिश्च मे नवविंशतिश्च मे,
नवविंशतिश्च मे एकत्रिंश्च्य मे, एकत्रिंश्च्य मे त्रयस्त्रिंशच्च्य मे
(यज्ञेन कल्पन्ताम् ।। यजुर्वेद। अध्याय 18 । मंत्र 24)

The above shloka talks about odd numbers 1, 3, 5, 7, 9, 11, 13, 15, 17, 19, 21, 23, 25, 27, 29, 31 and 33. The number mentioned here also forms an AP (Arithmetic Progression). Hence we can conclude here that mathematical concept of Odd numbers and Arithmetic progression were known to them. This is not the end of the story. Consider the next shloka of chapter 18:

चतस्रश्च मेऽष्टौ च मेऽष्टौ च मे द्वादश च मे, द्वादश च मे षोडश च मे,
षोडश च मे, विंशतिश्च मेऽष्टाविंशतिश्च मे, अष्टाविंशतिश्च द्वात्रिंशच्च्य मे,
द्वात्रिंशच्च्य मे षट्त्रिंशच्च्य मे, षट्त्रिंशच्च्य मे चत्वारिंशच्च्य मे,
चत्वारिंशच्च्य मे चतुश्चत्वारिंशच्च्य मे, चतुश्चत्वारिंशच्च्य मेऽष्टाचत्वारिंशच्च्य मे
(यज्ञेन कल्पन्ताम् ।। यजुर्वेद । अध्याय 18 । मंत्र 25)

The shloka talks about number in multiples of 4. The reference to numbers 4, 8, 12, 16, 20, 24, 32, 36, 40, 44 and 48 is evident in the above shloka. Simply put, the Vedas talk about what we call today Arithmetic Progression.

Another interesting fact about number 4 in the Vedas is that it is associated with the creator of universe Lord Brahma. Prof. S.S.N. Murthy in an article on 'A Note on the Ramayana' says that for a Hindu, only the Absolute, the Brahman, represented by the square is perfect and all that is on earth is imperfect. The square with its four sides, implies stability and unchanging character of the Absolute (Brahman), and is represented as a four-petal lotus seat of Brahma. The association of Lord Brahma with number 4 is also evident. Lord Brahma, the creator of universe, has four heads and four arms. The Puranas state that he sits on a four-petal lotus at the top of Meru Mountain which is surrounded by four continents and four seas. Besides, in Hindu mythology there are 4 Yugas—Satya Yug, Dwapar Yuga, Treta Yuga and Kali Yuga; 4 Phases of Life—Brahmacharya (before 24 Years), Grihasta (24–48), Vanaprasta (48–72), Sanyasa (72 and above); four seasons of three months each; four phases of the moon consisting of seven days each in a month, division of a day into four parts, etc.

The proper study of the above two shlokas reveal that they speak about even numbers, odd numbers, multiples and addition of numbers to form a new number, showing the richness of the holy books.

## Numbers in Decimal System

In the Yajur Veda, there are some bigger numbers and reference to numbers up to $10^{12}$. In Vajsaneyi Samhita, chapter 17, verse 2, the reference to numbers in ascending order is seen:

इमाः मे अग्ने इष्टकाः धेनवः सन्तु, एका च दशः च,
दशः च शतः च, शतः च सहस्र च,
सहस्राचायुते च, अयुतं च नियुतं च,

नियुतं च, नियुतं च प्रयुतं च,
प्रयुतं च अर्बुदं च, अर्बुदं च चन्यर्बुदं च,
समुद्रश्च मध्यं च, अंतश्चः परार्धश्च
एताः मे अग्ने इष्टकाः
धेनवः सन्तु अमुत्रामुष्मिन लोके।

Oh Agni! Let these bricks be milk-giving cows to me. Please give me one and ten and hundred and thousand, ten thousand and lakh and ten lakh and one crore and ten crore and hundred crore.

Eka (1), Dasa (10), Sata (100), Sahasra (1000), Ayuta (10,000), Niyuta (100,000), Prayuta (1,000,000), Arbuda (10,000,000), Nyarbuda (100,000,000), Samudra (1,000,000,000), Madhya (10000000000), Anta (100,000,000,000), and Parardha (1,000,000,000,000).

In Tayatri Sanhita of the Yajur Veda, numbers up to $10^{19}$ is mentioned. Continuing the list mentioned above, the name of the extended list goes like—$10^{13}$ उसस (Usas), $10^{14}$ व्युस्ति (Vyusti), $10^{15}$ देशयत (Desyat), $10^{16}$ उद्वत, $10^{17}$ उदित (UDIT), $10^{18}$ (सवर्ग savarg), and $10^{19}$ (लोक-lok).

It has been mentioned in the Puranas that the 18th number in succession, starting from 1 and inflating 10 times at—$110^{10}$ at every stage is called Pararddha.

एकं दश शतं चैव सहस्रायुतलक्षकम् ।
प्रयुतं काटिसंज्ञां चार्बुदमब्जं च खर्वकम्
निखर्वं च महापद्मं शंकुर्जलधिरेव च ।।
अन्त्यं मध्यं परार्धं च संज्ञा दशगिणोक्तरा ।
क्रमादुत्क्रमतो वापि योगः कार्योऽन्तरं तथा ।।

(ब्रह्मनारदीय पुराण 2/54 / 12—14)

एक (eka), दश (dasa), शत (sata), सहस्र (sahasra), अयुत (ayuta), लक्ष (laksa), प्रयुत (prayuta), कोटि (koti), अर्बुद (arbuda), पदम् (abja or padma), खर्व (kharva), निखर्व (nikharva), महापदम् (mahapadma), शंकु (sanku), समुद्र (samudra), अन्त्य (antya), मध्य (madhya), परार्ध

(parardha). These numbers are multiplies of 10.

The next number after Pararddha is Para, which is elaborately mentioned in the Mahabharata.

अयुतं प्रयुतं चैव शंखं पद्मं तथाबुर्दम्।
खर्व शंखं निखर्व च महापद्मां च कोटयः।।
मध्यं चैव परार्धं च सपरं चात्र पण्यताम्। (महाभारत सभापर्व 65/3 / 1-2)

The term Pararddha is used to mention the half lifetime of Lord Brahma and thus the complete life period is known as dwi-pararddha.

There is another passage in Veda presenting a list of powers of 10 starting from hundred to a trillion ($10^{12}$).

शताय स्वहा सहस्राय स्वाहायुताय स्वाहा नियुताय स्वाहा
प्रयुताय स्वाहाबुदाय स्वाहा न्यर्बुदाय स्वाहा समुद्राय स्वाहा,
मध्याय स्वाहान्ताय स्वाहा ............... परार्धाय स्वाहा।

(Hail to Hundred, Hail to Thousand, Hail to Hundred Million, hail to trillion.)

Bhaskaracharya in his book *Lilavati* talks about the place values of digits in the following stanzas:

एकादशशतसहस्रायुतलक्षप्रयुतकोटयः क्रमशः ।
अर्बुदमब्जं खर्वनिखर्वमहापद्माशंकवस्तस्मात् ।।
जलाधिश्चान्त्यं मध्यं परार्धमिति दशगुणोतरं संज्ञाः।
संख्यायाः स्थानानां व्यवहारार्थ कृताः पूर्वै।।

Positions of the digits from right to left are unit, ten, hundred, thousand, ten thousand, hundred thousand, million, ten million, hundred million, million, ten million, hundred million, billion (abja), kharva, nikharva, mahapadma, sanku, jaladhi, antya, madhya, parardha. The value of each digit on the left is 10 times that on the right.

According to the Taittiriya Upanishad, the magnitude of

ananda (bliss) obtained by human, Manushya Gandharva, Deva in magnitude Gandharva, Deva, Indra, Brihaspati, Prajapati and the revered Lord Brahma is greater by ten times than the previous one. The bliss obtained by Lord Brahma is mentioned in the 11th place. If we assume the bliss of human as 1 then the bliss of Manushya Gandharva is 10, Deva Gandharva is 100, Deva is 1000 and it goes ten times the previous one in succession and ends with the bliss given by Brahma which is equal to 10 raised to Power 11. Thus the enumeration of bliss would be 10 in unisons with 21. We consider Para, Parataranda Paratama as implicit designation from Mahabharata and consider 18th number as Pararddha, 19th as Para, 20th as Paratara and 21st as Paratama. Thus, the span of Vedic counting can expand till one accomplished by twenty zeros, which is very significant.

In the second mandala of the Rig Veda, numbers in the multiples of 10 have been described by means of the following shloka:

ता विंशत्या त्रिंशता या ह्वर्वाक् चत्वारिंशता हरिभिर्युजानः ।
ता पंचाशता सुरसेभिरिन्द्र षष्ट्या सप्तया सोम पेयम् ।।
अशीत्या नवत्या याह्यार्वाक् शतेन हरिभिरूह्यमानः । ।।ऋग्वेद।।

(O Indra, please come with twenty, thirty, forty horses ... with sixty, seventy? ---- carried by hundred horses.)

The holy Vedas don't only teach the number used at that very time but it also talks about the formation of big numbers by combining the numbers. The intermediate numbers have appropriate names given in the Vedas.

Ninety-four in the Rig Veda is termed as 90 + 4 and 19 is expressed as 20–1. In the Rig Veda, the number 3339 is spelled as three thousand, three hundred and thirty-nine.

त्रीणि शता त्रीसहस्राण्यग्निं त्रिंशश्च देवा नव चासपर्यन ।
औक्षन् घृतैरसृणन् बर्हिरस्मा .......

This shows that Vedic rishis were comfortable adding two, three or four numbers at a time.

3339 = 33 + 303 + 3003

That's not all. The Vedic rishis seemed to be comfortable multiplying numbers as well. Let's look at this sentence:

षष्टिं सहस्रानवतिं नव

This sentence talks about number 60099 and if you expand it as mentioned in the Rig Veda, you can see the formation of number using multiplication and addition.

60099 = 60 × 1000 + 90 + 9

Not all the people in Vedic time were quite obviously using the numeral system which made the basis of decimal system. The numeral system was the logical outcome of proceeding by multiples of ten. Thus, in an early system, 60,799 was denoted by the Sanskrit word sastim (sixty), shsara (thousand), sapta (seven) satani (hundred), navatim (nine ten times) and nava (nine). A scientifically-based vocabulary is needed to write such large words that involve addition, substraction and multiplication. Moreover it requires:

1.  the naming of the first nine digits (eka, dvi, tri, catur, pancha, sat, sapta, asta, nava);

2.  a second group of nine numbers obtained by multiplying each of the nine digits (as mentioned in previous point) by 10 (dasa, vimsat, trimsat, catvarimsat, panchasat, sasti, saptati, astiti, navati); and

3.  a group of numbers which are increasing integral powers of 10, starting with $10^2$ (satam sagasara, ayut, niyuta, prayuta, arbuda, nyarbuda, samudra, madhya, anta, parardha).

Most religious texts in the Vedic period were in the prose form and the numbers with two digits were written in a particular order: unit, ten.

12 = द्वादश
13 = त्रियोदश
14 = चतुर्दश
15 = पञ्चदश
23 = त्रिविंश
24 = चतुर्विंश

During ancient times, the unit digit is written first then the digit at ten's place. Therefore, it can be clearly said that Vedic scholars were aware of the fact that ordering of numbers should be in accordance with the rule unit, tens. Moreover, they were comfortable in writing numbers involving plus (+) and (−).

12 = 2 + 10 = dwa (2) + dash (10)
15 = 5 + 10 = panch (5) + dash (10)
19 = 20 − 1 = ekann (one less than) + vinshti (20)

Similarly, in case of numbers larger than two digits they used to write smaller numbers followed by the larger ones.

297 = त्रिहीन शतत्रय = 300 − 3

The Yajur Veda discusses bigger numbers up to the power $10^{12}$. S.S.N. Murthy in his article 'Number Symbolism in the Vedas', explains that there are several instances where Vedic rishis used number 1 to 5, 10 and multiple of tens. They also used numbers 90, 99, 100 and 1000 and its multiples. In the Vedas, the number 10, 100 or 1000 are used to mean many but the same time, the basic unit is referred as 10, 100 and 1000 to illustrate the fullness. The numbers 11, 33 and 34 also occur several times in the Vedas. There are a special references of number 7 in Vedas. सप्त तारा (Seven Stars), 7 colours of rainbow, 7 oceans are all created by God. As the legend goes, Lord Indra, the king of gods, cut down the foetus in the womb of Diti into 7 pieces and again each pieces into 7 parts. Agni, the god of fire, had 7 wives, mothers or sisters and could produce 7 flames. The Sun God had 7 horses to pull his heavenly chariot. In the Rig Veda there are 7 parts of the world, 7 seasons and 7 heavenly fortresses. This clearly shows the spiritual importance of number 7.

A child remains in his mother's womb for 9 months so number 9 has special significance, which is described later in this chapter.

The importance of number 9 has been discussed in the Puranas at length.

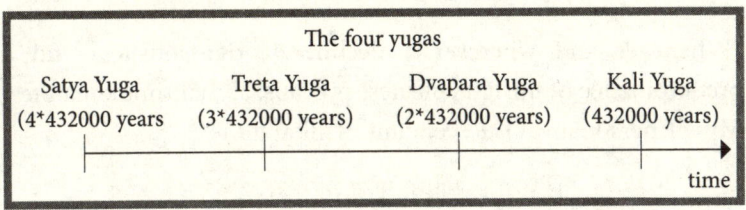

The four yugas

| Satya Yuga | Treta Yuga | Dvapara Yuga | Kali Yuga |
|---|---|---|---|
| (4*432000 years) | (3*432000 years) | (2*432000 years) | (432000 years) |

The Vishnu Purana, book 1, chapter 3, explains time management as follows:

- 2 Ayanas = 1 human year or 1 day of the devas
- 4,000 + 400 + 400 = 4,800 divine years (= 1,728,000 human years) = 1 Satya Yuga
- 3,000 + 300 + 300 = 3,600 divine years (= 1,296,000 human years) = 1 Treta Yuga
- 2,000 + 200 + 200 = 2,400 divine years (= 864,000 human years) = 1 Dvapara Yuga
- 1,000 + 100 + 100 = 1,200 divine years (= 432,000 human years) = 1 Kali Yuga

The unit sum of these number is divisible by 9.

Satya Yuga = 1 + 7 + 2 + 8 + 0 + 0 + 0 = 18
Treta Yuga = 1 + 2 + 9 + 6 + 0 + 0 + 0 = 18
Dvapara Yuga = 8 + 6 + 4 + 0 + 0 + 0 = 18
Kali Yuga = 4 + 3 + 2 + 0 + 0 + 0 = 18

If we write the same in terms of 1200 × 360 yr cosmic cycle, then the time periods reduce to 4, 3, 2 and 1 cycles of the above; the sum of which is 10.

The importance of the sum of cycle 10 referred here is also evident with the 10 incarnation of Lord Vishnu. Lord Vishnu incarnates on earth from time to time to eradicate evil forces and to restore dharma. In Bhagavad Gita, chapter 4, Lord Krishna says:

यदा यदा हि धर्मस्य ग्लानिर्भवति भारत।
अभ्युत्थानाधर्मस्य तदात्मानं सृजाम्यहम्।।7।।

(Whenever and wherever a decline of righteousness and a predominance of unrighteousness prevails, at that time I manifest Myself personally, O descendant of Bharata.)

परित्राणाय साधूनां विनाशाय च दुष्कृतम्।
धर्मसंस्थापनार्थाय सम्भवामि युगे युगे।।8।।

(For the protection of the devotees and the annihilation of the miscreants and to fully establish righteousness, I appear millennium after millenium.)

The 10 avatars or incarnations of Lord Vishnu are described in Vishnu Purana as:

(1)  Matsya (मत्सय)—Fish
(2)  Kachap (कच्छप)—Tortoise
(3)  Varaha (शूकर)—Boar
(4)  Narasimha (नरसिंह)—half man, half lion
(5)  Vamana (वामन)—human-lion
(6)  Parashurama (परशुराम)
(7)  Rama (राम)
(8)  Krishna (कृष्ण)
(9)  Buddha (बुद्ध)
(10) Kalki (कल्कि)—Mighty warrior

Poet Jayadeva in his book *Gita Govinda* has described the 10 incarnations of Lord Vishnu in detail:

प्रलयपयोधिजले धृतवानसि वेदम्।

विहितवहित्रचरित्रमखेदम् ।
केशव, धृतमीनशरीर, जय जगदीश हरे ।1।

(O Kesava [Vishnu]! In the form of Fish, Holding the Vedas like a vessel undeflected from its course in the deluge to preserve the knowledge of Vedas, You took the incarnation of Fish! Praise be to Jagadish! Lord of the universe!)

क्षितिरतिविपुलतरे तव तिष्ठति पृष्ठे
धरणिधरणकिणचक्रगरिष्ठे ।
केशव, धृतकच्छपरूप, जय जगदीश हरे ।2।

(O Kesava [Vishnu]! In the form of Tortoise [kacchaparupa], On your broad and vast back the world rests, creating circular marks. Praise be to Jagadish! Lord of the universe!)

वसति दशनशिखरे धरणी तव लग्ना
शशिनि कलंककलेव निमग्ना ।
केशव, धृतशूकररूप, जय जगदीश हरे ।3।

(O Kesava [Vishnu]! In the form of the Boar [sukara]! Fixed on the tips of your tusks the earth did dwell peacefully, resembling the digit of the moon. Praise be to Jagadish! Lord of the universe!)

तव करकमवरे नखमद्भुतशृङ्गम्
दलितहिरण्यकशिपुतनुभृङ्गम् ।
केशव, धृतनरहरिरूप, जय जगदीश हरे ।4।

(O Kesava [Vishnu]! In the form of Man-Lion [Naraharirupa]! Your lotus hands with sharp nails became wonderful claws that tore and shredded the body of demon Hiranyakasyapu protecting your devotee Prahlada. Praise be to Jagadish! Lord of the universe!)

छलयसि विक्रमणे बलिमद्भुतवामन,
पदनखनीरजनितजनपावन ।
केशव, धृतवामनरूप, जय जगदीश हरे ।5।

(O Kesava [Vishnu]! In the form of the Dwarf [Vamana] You cleverly deceived the King of the world, Bali. Cleanser of the people through the sweat of your toenails. Praise be to Jagadish! Lord of the universe!)

क्षत्रियरूधिरमये जगदपगतपापम्
स्नपयसि पयसि शमितभवतापम्
केशव, धृतभृगुपतिरूप, जय जगदीश हरे |6|

(O Kesava [Vishnu]! In the form of the Lord of Bhrigus [Parshurama], You have rid the earth of its tyrannous rulers, thus purifying it of sin and destroying the suffering of the world. Praise be to Jagadish! Lord of the universe!)

वितरसि दिक्षु रणे दिक्पतिकमनीयं
दशमुखमौलिबलि रमणीयम् |
केशव, धृतरामरूप, जय जगदीश हरे |7|

(O Kesava [Vishnu]! In the form of Lord Rama to uphold dharma or righteousness, You spread the ten heads of Ravana in the four directions, rendering the guardians there of resplendent! O Kesava! You assumed the form of Rama! Praise be to Jagadish! Lord of the universe!)

बहसि वपुषि विशदे वसनं जलदाभम्।
हलहतिभीतिमिलितयमुनाभम्
केशव, धृतहलधररूप, जय जगदीश हरे |8|

(O Kesava [Vishnu]! In the form of Balarama, the plough bearer! You wear on your glowing body garments the colour of the cloud, blue like the river Yamuna, flowing because of the fear of your plough! O Kesava! You assumed the form of Balarama. Praise be to Jagadish! Lord of the universe.)

निन्दसि यज्ञविधेरहह श्रुतिजातम्
सदयह्रदयदर्शितपशुधातम् |

केशव, धृतबुद्धरूप, जय जगदीश हरे ।9।

(O Kesava [Vishnu]! In the form of Buddha, the enlightened one! Out of compassion in your heart you have condemned the ritualistic fraction of the Vedas proclaiming the killing of innocent animals. Praise be to Jagadish! Lord of the universe!)

म्लेच्छनिबहनिधने कलयसि करवालं
धूमकेतुमिव किमपि करालम् ।
केशव, धृतकल्किशरीर, जय जगदीश हरे ।10।

(O Kesava [Vishnu]! In the form of the severe Kalkii to destroy the wicked, You carry a comet like sword in your hand, trailing a succession of disasters upon the wicked and evil. Praise be to Jagadish! Lord of the universe!)

*The ten avatars of Lord Vishnu (clockwise from top-left)*
*Matsya, Kurma, Varaha, Vamana, Krishna in centre, Kalki,*
*Buddha, Parshurama, Rama and Narasimha. Painting currently*
*in the Victoria and Albert Museum. (Source: Wikipedia)*

Besides that, the Linga Purana describes the 12 jyotirlingas of Shiva (Lord Shiva's appearances in the form of light). It is believed that a person can see these lingas as columns of fire piercing through the earth after he attains a higher level of spiritual enlightenment.

सौराष्ट्रे सोमनाथं च श्रीशैले मल्लिकार्जुनम् ।
उज्जयिन्यां महाकालमोङ्कारममलेश्वरम् ॥
परल्यां वैद्यनाथं च डाकिन्यां भीमशंकरम् ।
सेतुबन्धे तु रामेशं नागेशं दारूकावने ॥
वाराणस्यां तु विश्वेशं त्र्यंबकं गौतमीतटे ।
हिमालये तु केदारं घुश्मेशं च शिववालये ॥

The 12 jyotirlingas are Somnath in Gujarat, Mallikarjuna at Srisailam in Andra Pradesh, Mahakaleswar at Ujjain in Madhya Pradesh, Omkareshwar in Madhya Pradesh, Kedarnath in the Himalayas, Bhimashankar in Maharashtra, Viswanath at Varanasi in Uttar Pradesh, Triambakeshwar in Maharashtra, Vaidyanath at Deoghar in Jharkhand, Aundha Nagnath at Aundha in Hingoli in Maharashtra, Rameshwar at Rameswaram in Tamil Nadu and Grishneshwar at Ellora near Aurangabad in Maharashtra.

## Time Measurement

According to the Vedas time is equal to Kala. It unites procession, recession and stasis.

कालो गतिर्निवति स्थितिः समदाधहति

(Time moves in every situation.)

कालः पचति भूतानि, कालः संहरते प्रजा।
कालः सुप्तेषु जागति, कालो हि दुरतिक्रमः ॥
(महाभारत–स्त्री पर्व 2, 22)

(Time digest all things, Time kills all that are born, Time is awake while all else sleeps, Time is insurmountable.)

This shloka is said by Vidura to the King Dhritrasthra in Mahabharta that shows the strength of time.

There is a passage in the Bhagvata Purana which deals about the time measurement in ancient times:

Taking his own daughter, Revati, Kakudmi went to Lord Brahma in Brahmaloka, and enquired about a husband for her. When Kakudmi arrived there, Lord Brahma was engaged in hearing musical performances by the Gandharvas and had not a moment to talk with him. Therefore Kakudmi waited, and at the end of the performance he saluted Lord Brahma and made his desire known. After hearing his words, Lord Brahma laughed loudly and said to Kakudmi, 'O King, all those whom you may have decided within the core of your heart to accept as your son-in-law have passed away in the course of time. Twenty-seven chaturyugas have already passed. Those upon whom you may have decided are now gone, and so are their sons, grandsons and other descendants. You cannot even hear about their names.'

In Manusmriti, chapter 1, there is a shloka which divides a day into smaller time units.

निमिषे दश चाष्टौ च काष्ठा त्रिषत्तु ताः कला ।
त्रिंशत्कला मुहूर्तः स्यादहोरात्रं तु तावतः ॥

According to this shloka, the time taken by a blink is called Nimisha which is the smaller unit of time.

18 Nimisha = 1 Kastha
30 Kastha = 1 kala
30 Kala = 1 Muhurt

30 Muhurt = 1 Day

A discourse on time management is also described in the Vedas. In the Rig Veda Mandala 10, Sukta 14 mantra 1 × 3 says that the time pervades all the articles of the universe and controls them. Time is the cause of the creation, sustenance and destruction of all matters of Universe.

On the other hand, Yoga Shastra Chapter 3 and Shloka 52 states—the minutest part of the time is kshann, i.e. a moment of time. Kshann cannot be further divided. After passing of a kshann, another kshann transcend. In between te two kshanns there is no time gap. Time flows continuously.

According to the Surya Siddhanta, time has both virtual and practical divisions. The former is called murta—मूर्त (embodied) and latter amurta—अमूर्त (virtual or unembodied).

लोकोनामन्तकृत् कालः कालोऽन्यः कलनात्मकः ।
स द्विधा स्थूलसूक्ष्मत्वान्मूर्तश्चामूर्त उच्यते ॥

Time has two types—one that kills the living things and another that counts. The counting time can further be classified as murta-embodied and another amurta-unembodied.

Vedic astronomy gives a very detailed division of the time up to the lowest sub division level of prana (respiration), which is a time lapse of four seconds. The Surya Siddhanta delineates that which begins with prana is called real and what begins with tuti (atoms) is called unreal. The lowest division prana is equal to 1 minute of circle. A circle has 360 divisions each of 1 degree so the prana is one part of the 360 divisions.

प्राणादिः कथितो मूर्तस्त्रुट्याद्योऽमूर्तसंज्ञकः
षड्भिः प्राणैर्विनाडीस्यात्तत्षष्ट्या नाडिका स्मृता।
नाडीषष्ट्या तु नाक्षत्रमहोरात्रं प्रकीर्तितम्
तत् त्रिशता भवेन्मासः सावनोऽर्कोदयैस्तथा ॥

According to the above shloka in the Surya Siddhanata,

6 Prana = 1 Vinadi (Pala) = 24 seconds

60 Pala = 1 Nadi = 24 minutes

60 Nadis = 1 Ahoratra

30 Ahoratra = 1 month

According to modern standards, 24 hours make one day and one night, 1 nadi or daṇḍa is equal to 24 minutes, 1 vinadi is equal to 24 seconds, 1 prana is equal to 4 seconds, 1 nimisha is equal to 88.889 milliseconds, 1 tatpara is equal to 2.96296 milliseconds and finally 1 truṭi is equal to 29.6296 microseconds or 33,750th part of second. It is really amazing that the Indian astronomers, such a long time ago, could conceive and measure such a small interval of time like truti. It should be mentioned here that, 1 unit of prana is the time an average healthy man needs to complete one respiration or to pronounce ten long syllables called guravaksara.

This is not all you may find in Vedic literature. The other divisions of time are described here in a tabular form:

| Unit | Definition | Equivalence |
| --- | --- | --- |
| Truti (त्रुटि) | | 0.031μs |
| Renu (रेणु) | 60 truti | 1.85 μs |
| Lava (लव) | 60 Renu | 0.11 ms |
| Liksaka (लीक्षक) | 60 Lava | 6.67 ms |
| Lipta (लिप्ता) | 60 Liksaka | 0.4 second |
| Pala/Vighati (पल / विघटि) | 60 Lipta | 24 seconds |
| Ghati / Nadi / Dandi (घटि / नाडि / दंड) | 60 Vighati | 24 minutes |
| Danda / Muhurta (दंड / मुहुर्त) | 2 Ghati | 48 minutes |
| Naksatra Ahoratam (नक्षत्र अहरोत्रम) | 60 Ghati | 24 hours |

An alternate system has been discussed at length at the Vishnu Purana, book 1, chapter 3, which is as follows:

- 100 Truti = 1 Tatpara

- 30 Tatpara = 1 Nimesha
- 15 Nimeshas = 1 Káshthá
- 30 Káshthás = 1 Kala
- 30 Kalas = 1 Kala
- 12 Kshaṅa = 1 Muhúrtta
- 30 Muhúrttas = 1 day (24 hours)
- 30 days = 1 month
- 6 months = 1 Ayana
- 2 Ayanas = 1 year or 1 day (day + night) of the gods

Small units are also discussed in Vedas. Let's have a look at them in accordance with the present time scale.

| Unit | Definition | Equivalence |
|---|---|---|
| Paramanu (परमाणु) | | 26.3 μs |
| Anu (अणु) | 2 Paramanu | 57.7 μs |
| Trasarenu | 3 Anu | 158 μs |
| Truti (त्रुटि) | 3 Trasarenu | 474 μs |
| Vedha (वेध) | 100 Truti | 47.4 ms |
| Lava (लव) | 3 Vedha | 0.14 second |
| Nimesa (निमिषा) | 3 Lava | 0.43 second |
| Ksana (क्षण) | 3 Nimesha | 1.28 second |
| Kastha | 5 Ksana | 6.4 second |
| Laghu (लधु) | 15 Kastha | 1.6 minutes |
| Danda (दंड) | 15 Laghu | 24 minutes |
| Muhurta (मुहूर्त) | 2 Danda | 48 minutes |
| Ahoratram (अहोरात्रम्) | 30 Muhurta | 24 hours |
| Masa (मास) | 30 Ahoratram | 30 days |
| Ritu (ऋतु) | 2 Masa | 2 Months |
| Ayana (आयना) | 3 Ritus | 6 Months |
| Samvatsara (संवतसार) | 2 Ayana | 360 Days |

There is a shloka in the Surya Siddhanta which divides the

whole year in 12 months or 360 days. These days are divided in accordance with the lunar and solar calendars.

ऐन्दवस्तिथिभिस्तद्द्वत् संक्रान्तया सौर उच्यते।
मासैर्द्वादशभिर्वषै दिव्यं तदह उच्यते।।

As 1 lunar month has 30 days so does 1 solar month has 30 days. Twelve months make one year and 1 year makes one divya day. This clearly indicates that in Vedic Period 1 year = 12 × 30 = 360 days. The days and nights (Ahoratra) of god and demon were opposite to each other. The days for god as were the nights for demon and vice versa.

Samvatsara is a Sanskrit term for 'year'. In Hindu tradition, there are 60 samvatsaras, each of which has a name. Once all 60 samvatsaras are over, the cycle starts over again. The 60 samvatsaras are divided into 3 groups of 20 samvatsaras each. The first 20 from Prabhava to Vyaya are attributed to Lord Brahma. The next 20 from Sarvajit to Parabhava to Vishnu and the last 20 to Shiva. The 60 samvatsaras are:

| 1. Prabhava | 16. Chitrabhānu | 31. Hemalambin | 46. Paritāpin |
|---|---|---|---|
| 2. Vibhava | 17. Svabhānu | 32. Vilambin | 47. Pramādin |
| 3. Shukla | 18. Tārana | 33. Vikārin | 48. Ānanda |
| 4. Pramoda | 19. Pārthiva | 34. Shārvari | 49. Rākshasa |
| 5. Prajāpati | 20. Vyaya | 35. Plava | 50. Anala |
| 6. Āngirasa | 21. Sarvajit | 36. Shubhakrit | 51. Pingala |
| 7. Shrīmukha | 22. Sarvadhārin | 37. Shobhana | 52. Kālayukti |
| 8. Bhāva | 23. Virodhin | 38. Krodhin | 53. Siddhārthin |
| 9. Yuvan | 24. Vikrita | 39. Vishvāvasu | 54. Raudra |
| 10. Dhātri | 25. Khara | 40. Parābhava | 55. Durmati |
| 11. Īshvara | 26. Nandana | 41. Plavanga | 56. Dundubhi |
| 12. Bahudhānya | 27. Vijaya | 42. Kīlaka | 57. Rudhirodgārin |
| 13. Pramāthin | 28. Jaya | 43. Saumya | 58. Raktāksha |
| 14. Vikrama | 29. Manmatha | 44. Sādhārana | 59. Krodhana |
| 15. Vrisha | 30. Durmukha | 45. Virodhikrit | 60. Kshaya |

The time unit larger than a year is called yuga and 12,000 years of divya year is called 1 Chaturyuga or Mahayuga.

तद्द्वादशसहस्राणि चतुर्युगमुदाहृतम् ।
सूर्याब्दसङ्ख्यया द्वित्रिसागरैरयुताहतैः ।।
सन्ध्यासन्ध्यांशसहितं विज्ञेय तच्चतुर्युगम् ।
कृतादीनां व्यवस्थेयं धर्मपादव्यवस्थया ।।

(सूर्यसिद्धांत 1.15–16)

In the Surya Siddhanta, it is clearly mentioned that 1 Mahayuga is equal to 12,000 divya years and as stated earlier that there is 360 solar years in a divya years.

Hence, $12000 \times 360 = 4320000$ years makes a Mahayuga.

It has also been stated in the scripture that there are 4 yugas namely—Sat Yuga, Treta Yuga, Dwapar Yuga and Kali Yuga.

युगस्य दशमो भागश्चतुस्त्रिद्वेकसंगुणः ।
क्रमात् कृतयुगादीनां षष्ठांशः संध्ययोः स्वकः ।।

This shloka states that when you multiply the tenth part of a Mahayuga and multiply it by 1, 2, 3 and 4 you get Sat Yuga, Treta Yuga, Dwapara Yuga and Kali Yuga.

1 Mahayuga = 12000 divya years
One-tenth of Mahayuga = 1200 divya years
$1200 \times 1 = 1200$ divya years $= 1200 \times 360 = 432000$ years
$1200 \times 2 = 2400$ divya years $= 2400 \times 360 = 864000$ years
$1200 \times 1 = 1200$ divya years $= 3600 \times 360 = 1296000$ years
$1200 \times 1 = 1200$ divya years $= 1200 \times 360 = 432000$ years
Moreover, I Manvantara is 71 Mahayugas i.e.,
1 Mahayuga = 308,448,000 years

This time is approximately equal to the time taken by the sun to complete one revolution around the centre of galaxy.

1 Kalpa = 4,320,000,000 years is the time span equal to the age of the universe.

## Fraction

There are instance in the Rig Veda where fractions have been used—अर्द्ध–Ardhya (1/2), त्रिपाद–Tripad (3/4), पाद–paad (1/4), कुष्ठ–Kushtha (1/12), कला–Kala (1/16).

ज्येष्ठ आह चमसा दवा करेति
कनीयान तरीन कर्णवामेत्य आह।
कनिष्ठ आह चतुरस करेति तवष्ट
रभवस् तत पनयद वचो वः ।।

In Sulva Sutra, ansh (अंश) / bhag (भाग) has been used as triansh (त्रिअंश) or tribhag (त्रिभाग) for 1/3, pancham (पंचम) for 1/5 and dwadash (द्वादश) for 1/12. There were special methods to write mixed fractions as seen in Sulbha Sutra like—अर्धाष्टम् ardhastam (7½), अर्धनवम् ardhanavam (8½), त्रयस्त्रष्ट trayastratha (3⅗) were common words found. In the treatment of fractions, Mahavira was the first amongst the Indian mathematicians, who used the method of Least Common Multiple to shorten the process and he called it Niruddha. He defined it as 'The niruddha is obtained by means of continued multiplication of all the possible common factors of the denominators and all their ultimate quotients.'

## Infinity

The concept of infinity was also known during Vedic times. Words like ananta, purnam, aditi and asamkhyata have been used in the Vedas. The Mahavaipulya Buddhavatamsaka Sutra, also known as the Avatamsaka Sutra, contains a description of an 'incalculable' number divined to describe the innumerable names and forms of the principal deities Vishnu and Shiva. In Brihadaranyaka Upanishad, the number of mysterious powers of Indra is defined as ananta.

पूर्णमदः पूर्णमिदं पूर्णात् पूर्णमुदच्यते ।
पूर्णस्य पूर्णमादाय पूर्णमेवावशिष्यते ॥

(The 'Complete Whole', that is said here must contain everything both within and beyond our experience, otherwise He cannot be complete. When the 'Complete Whole' is taken away from the 'Complete', what remains is the 'Complete Whole' itself.)

From infinity is born infinity. When infinity is taken out of infinity only infinity remains.

In modern notations:

$$\infty + \infty = \infty \qquad\qquad \infty - \infty = \infty$$

अनेकबाहूदरवक्त्रनेत्रं पश्यामि त्वां सर्वतोऽनन्तरूपम् ।
नान्तं न मध्यं न पुनस्तवादिं पश्यामि विश्वेश्वर विश्वरूप ॥

(Shrimad Bhagwad Gita, Chapter-11, Shloka-16)

Sri Madhvacarya of Brahma Vaisnava Sampradaya, in his commentary on the above shloka, writes that the word aneka means innumerable. In Lord Krishna's Visvarupa or divine universal form, witnessed multitudinous arms, faces, stomachs and eyes unlimitedly. The word visva denotes without any restrictions. Everything regarding Lord Krishna is infinitely endless and complete in all manifestations. The compound word ananta-rupam means innumerable forms and it also means that His forms are unlimited.

अनादिमध्यान्तमनन्तवीर्यम् अनंतबाहु शशिसूर्यनेत्रम् ।
पश्यामि त्वां दीप्तहुताशवक्त्रं स्वतेजसा विश्वमिदं तपन्तम् ॥

(Shrimad Bhagwad Gita, Chapter-11, Shloka-19)

(I see You without beginning, middle or end; of infinite energy with unlimited arms, with eyes like the sun and the moon with blazing fire in your mouths, heating the universe by Your glorious radiance.)

This shloka clearly defines that infinity has no beginning,

middle or end which in mathematical language can be said that any operation on infinity doesn't affect its value.

In 1638, Galileo wrote in *Two New Sciences*: 'So far as I see we can only infer that the totality of all numbers is infinite, that the number of squares is infinite, and that the number of their roots is infinite; neither is the number of squares less than the totality of all numbers, nor the latter greater than the former; and finally the attributes "equal", "greater", and "less", are not applicable to infinite, but only to finite, quantities.'

Big numbers that go up to infinity have been discussed in Buddhism and Jainism.

## Concept of Zero

In 1912, Prof. G.B. Halsted said, 'The importance of the creation of the zero mark can never be exaggerated. No single mathematical creation has been more potent for the general on go of intelligence and power.'

The discovery of 0 in mathematics is one of the greatest achievements of mankind. Its discovery has helped science to reach its current status and mathematicians to write big numbers without any confusion. It has also helped develop the place-value system among other things.

'The ingenious method of expressing every possible number using a set of ten symbols (each symbol having a place value and an absolute value) emerged in India. The idea seems so simple nowadays that its significance and profound importance is no longer appreciated. Its simplicity lies in the way it facilitated calculation and placed arithmetic foremost amongst useful inventions. The importance of this invention is more readily appreciated when one considers that it was beyond the two greatest men of Antiquity, Archimedes and Apollonius said Pierre-Simon

Laplace, the influential French scholar.

The number 0 is the creation of an Indian is known to the world, a place but very few people know that in the Vedas it is used as a symbol to show unavailability. In the Atharva Veda, the शून्यैषी (sunyashi) has been used for a person willing to find unavailable object.

शून्यैषी निर्ऋते याजगन्धोत्तिष्ठाराते प्रपत मेह रंस्था

(अथर्ववेद 14.2.19)

The concept of shunya was originally conceived as the symbol of Brahman, expressing the sum of all distinct forms. Shri Ashutosh Maharaj in 'Zero, Mathematics and Consciousness' published on 27 February 2012 in *The Times of India*, wrote, 'In the Brihadaranyaka Upanishad, Sage Yagyavalkya was asked by his pupils to explain the nature of Brahmn, Universal Consciousness. The sage replied: "Neti Neti neither This nor That—such is Brahmn".'

This definition sounds enigmatic. But within this mysterious concept lies the profound philosophy of existence, which can be understood in terms of mathematics. If we look for a mathematical numeral equivalent to the Upanishadic 'Neti Neti', it is zero, because zero is neither this nor that; it is neither positive nor negative. Therefore, the Vedas proclaim: 'Aum Kham Brahmn', meaning Brahmn is shunya or zero! Hence, Brahman = 0.

The symbol of zero and the decimal system of notation is described in the Atharva Veda and we have given a fair description on it. As mentioned above, during the Vedic era people could count in the multiples of 10 up to $10^{18}$ and it could not have been possible without the knowledge of the fact that if a zero is put in front of a number it increases its value by ten times.

Panini's *Astadhyayi* (500 BC) has the reference to zero and word lopa has been used fot it.

अदर्शनं लोपः । (1.1.60)

(The importance of zero has been considered in the Vedas, Puranas and other religious literature.)

मूले शून्यं विजानीयात् । शून्यं वै परं ब्रह्म । (गणेशपूर्वतापिन्युपनिषत् 3 / 1)

(Everyone is born from the sunya, and sunya is the ultimate Brahma.)

The above statement proves 0 as the basic numeral and its Supreme being-like attribute.

At another instance in *Tejobindupanisat,* zero is considered as the subtle form of Atman. It is the whole form as in one etc., and is also devoid of whole or whole-less.

शून्यात्मा सूक्ष्मरूपात्मा विश्वात्मा विश्वहीनकः ।
देवात्मा देवहीनात्मा मेयात्मा मानवर्जितः ।। (तेजोबिन्दूपनिषत् 4 / 43)

(While being able to manifest itself by elevating to the form of one it is also the terminal of one being existent it is demonstrable, while being self-evident it is causeless.)

In Srimad Bhavat Gita 10/14/23, the importance of zero has been described as:

पूर्णोऽद्वयो मुक्त उपाधितोऽमृतः

Zero is apparently like Lord Brahma. It is free from all attributes and is imperishable.

Swami Niscalananda Saraswati of Govardhan Matha Puri in his book *Ganitacintamani* writes zero as selfless number because you get 0 when you subtract the number from itself.

1 − 1 = 0

2 − 2 = 0 etc...

The earliest known reference of 0 is in *Chandasastra* written by Pingala in 200 BC. Let's analyze the shloka used by him:

गायत्रे षड्संख्यामर्धेऽपनीते द्वयड्के अवशिष्ट स्रयस्तेषु ।
रूपमपनीय द्वयड.काधः शुन्यं स्थाप्यम् ।।

In Gayatri Chandas, one pada has six letters. (A Gayatri Mantra has four padas with twenty-four syllables. Please refer to the section discussed later on Gayatri Mantra for more detail). When this number is divided into halves; it becomes three, remove one from it and make it half to get one. Remove one from it and you get zero. Mathematically it can be represented as:

$$0 = \frac{1}{2} \left\{ \frac{1}{2} \text{ of } 6 - 1 \right\} - 1$$

*A dedication tablet in a rock-cut Vishnu temple in Gwalior built in 876 AD. The number 270 seen in the inscription features the oldest extant zero in India. (Photos courtesy: Bill Casselman; 'Understanding Ancient Indian Mathematics', The Hindu, dated 26 December 2011)*

The above image is of Rama rock found in Gwalior, Madhya Pradesh from where the number was taken. This rock is situated in Vishnu Temple, which was built around 876 AD, where the numbers 270 and 50 are written as we write today; the only difference is that the 0 is smaller and slightly raised. The description is as follows—

'They have planted a garden 187 by 270 hastas which would produce enough flowers to allow 50 garlands per day to be given to the local temple.'

*Vishnu Temple of Gwalior*
*(Source: http://www.gettyimages.in/pictures/vishnu-temple-gwalior-*
*madhya-pradesh-india-news-photo-558029059)*

D.E. Smith, a renowned mathematics historian, says, 'Without it the Hindu numerals would be no better than many others, since the distinguishing feature of our present system is its place value. The earliest undoubted occurence of zero in India is seen in an inscription of 876 AD, at Gwalior. In this inscription 50 and 270 are both written with zeros. We have evidence however that a place value was recognized at an earlier period so that the zero had probably been known for a long time... We simply know that the world left the need of a better number system and that the zero appeared in India as early as the 9th century and probably some time before that and was very likely a Hindu invention.'

## About Seven Colours of Light

अधुक्षत्पिप्युषीमिषमुर्ज सप्तमदीमारी ।
सूर्यस्य सप्त रश्मिभिः ।। (ऋग्वेद 8 .72. 16)

(The seven rays of the sun are falling, there I live with my family. This clearly shows that people at that time knew that the colour white is the mixture of 7 colours and here sun which is white in colour contains the 7 colours.)

In the Rig veda, light is explained as a source of energy or source of our life. In a hymn of the Rig veda (5.45.9) a description that 'seven horses draw the chariot of the sun, tied by snakes' clearly proves the seven colour of a light.

## Speed of Light

In the Rig veda, following shloka's state about the speed of light which is nearly about of modern value of 186,282.397 miles / seconds:

तथा च स्मर्यते योजनानां सहस्रे द्वे द्वे शते द्वे च चोजने एकेन
निमिषार्धेन क्रममाण नमोऽस्तु ते इति ।। ऋग्वेद ।।

(O sun, bow to you, you who transverse 2202 yojana in half a nimisha.)

Sayanacarya who was a minister in the court of Bukka of the great Vijayanagar Empire of Karnataka (in early 14th century) describes the speed of light in terms of the modern value in a commentary.

In the verse, Sun's light speed is measured with the help of units called Yojan & Nimesh. This verse explain that sunlight moves 2202 Yojans in Half Nimesh.

According to the Mahabharata, Shanti Parva, half a *nimisha* is equal to 8/75 seconds, which makes the total velocity of light to be 186413.22 miles per second, which is very close to the modern value.

## Gayatri Mantra and its meaning

The Gayatri Mantra was revealed by Rishi Yagna Valkya. This

is taken from the Rig Veda (3.62.10). This mantra is also called Savitri Mantra which is related to the worship of sun. The Gaytari Mantra has been bestowed with the greatest importance in Vedic literature—it is called the mother of the Vedas.

ॐ भूर्भुवः स्वः ।
तत्सवितुर्वरेण्यं ।
भर्गो देवस्यं धीमहि ।
धियो यो नः प्रचोदयात् ।।

[Om bhur bhuvah svaha, Tat savitur varenyam
Bhargo devasya dheemahi, dhiyo yo nah prachodayat]

(O God! You are Omnipresent, Omnipotent and Almighty; You are all Light. You are all Knowledge and Bliss. You are Destroyer of fear, You are Creator of this Universe, You are the Greatest of all. We bow and meditate upon Your light. You guide our intellect in the right direction.)

There are 24 aksharas in the Gayatri Mantra and since this mantra is related to the Sun god it can be inferred that it takes 24 hours to move the earth around the sun. Twenty-four is the time code. The other query that can be raised is that why did our ancestors select 24 hours to denote a day and why not 20 or 30 hours?

It is also said that one should not read the Gayatri more than 3,000 times and that too in three sessions in a day with maximum 1,000 times per session. Let's understand the basic reasoning behind it, which I found in a blog by Prashanth Rajarao.

Since the Gayartri mantra consists of 24 aksharas so

$24 \times 1000$ times = 24,000 in a session

$24000 \times 3$ session = 72,000 in a day

Our body is said to comprise of 72,000 nerves (naadis) and the Gayatri Mantra charges each nerves with its recitation. As excess charge can be fatal for the body, so the chanting of this mantra is restricted to 3,000 times.

The Gayatri Mantra is one of the keynotes to the transformation of consciousness and is an identical vibration to the vital force in nature. The 24 syllables of this mantra are as follows:

| 1. | 'tat' | — | tapini | — | fruitfulness |
| 2. | 'sa' | — | saphalata | — | valour |
| 3. | 'vi' | — | visshwa | — | perseverance |
| 4. | 'tur' | — | tushti | — | welfare |
| 5. | 'va' | — | varada | — | yoga |
| 6. | 're' | — | revati | — | love |
| 7. | 'ni' | — | sukshma | — | wealth |
| 8. | 'yam' | — | jnana | — | lustre |
| 9. | 'bhar' | — | bharga | — | protection |
| 10. | 'go' | — | gomati | — | wisdom |
| 11. | 'de' | — | devika | — | subjugation |
| 12. | 'va' | — | varahi | — | allegiance |
| 13. | 'sya' | — | simhani | — | determination |
| 14. | 'dhi' | — | dhyana | — | life |
| 15. | 'ma' | — | maryada | — | time |
| 16. | 'hi' | — | sphutaa | — | penance |
| 17. | 'dhi' | — | medha | — | forecast |
| 18. | 'yo' | — | yogamaya | — | alertness |
| 19. | 'yo' | — | yogini | — | production |
| 20. | 'nah' | — | dhanin | — | protection |
| 21. | 'pra' | — | prabhava | — | idealism |
| 22. | 'cho' | — | ushma | — | adventure |
| 23. | 'da' | — | drishya | — | discrimination |
| 24. | 'at' | — | niranjana | — | service |

## Numbers in Ramayana

The Ramayana, revered epic in the Hindu religion, was first

written by Maharshi Valmiki and later written in prose in Awadhi language by Sant Tulsidas. The event and story of the Ramayana took place in Treta Yuga, the second of the four yugas. It depicts the duties of relationships and portrays ideal characters like the ideal father, the ideal servant, the ideal brother, the ideal wife and the ideal king. The Ramayana consists of 24,000 verses in 7 parts called 7 kandas with 500 sargas (cantos) and tells the story of Rama (an avatar of Lord Vishnu).

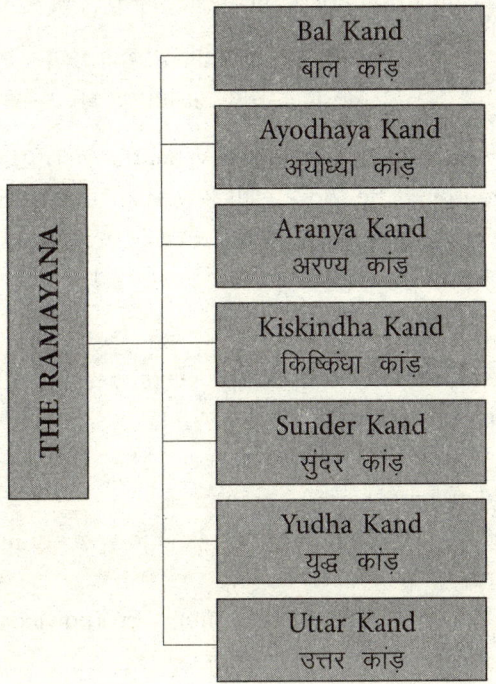

The Ramayana of Maharaishi Valmiki dates back to approximately 5th to 4th BC. It is a tale that narrates the virtuous journey of to annihilate vice.

As far as mathematical knowledge in this holy book is concerned, there are several poems that speak about the mathematical numbers as we use today. In Sundara Kanda of the

Valmiki Ramayana, there is an instance when Hanuman describes
Rama's bodily feature in number to Sita in Ashok Vatika where Sita
was in captivity of Ravana in Lanka and Hanuman reached there in
search of Mata Sita and Sita asks about the appearance and qualities
of Rama and Lakshmana to establish the identity of Hanuman.
In Sarga 35, of the Sundara Kanda shlokas 17 to 21, Hanuman
describes the body parts of Lord Ram. Hanuman described the
bodily features of Lord Rama to Sita, held in captivity in Ashok
Vatika by means of numbers such as 2, 3, 4, 5, 6, 9, 10 and 14.

यजुः वेद विनीतः च वेदविद्भिः सुपूजितः ।
धनुः वेदे च वेदे च वेद अन्येषु च निष्ठितः ।। (5–35–14)

Rama was well-trained in the Yajur Veda, the sacrificial Veda. He
is highly honoured by those well-versed in the Vedas. He was
skilled in the Dhanur veda, the science of archery, other Vedas
and six limbs of Vedangas.

The six limbs of Vedanga are—

1. Siksha (शिक्षा)—the science of proper articulation and
   pronounciation
2. Chandas (छंद)—the metre
3. Vyakarana (व्याकरण)—grammar
4. Nirukta (निरुक्ता)—the explanation of difficult Vedic
   words
5. Jyotisha (ज्योतिष)—the astronomy or knowledge of Vedic
   calendar
6. Kalpa (कल्प)—the ceremonial represented by a large
   number of Sura works

त्रिस्थिरः त्रिप्रलम्बः च त्रिसमः त्रिषु च उन्नतः ।
त्रिवलीवान् त्र्यवनतः चतुःव्यङ्गः त्रिशीर्षवान् ।। (5–35–17)

He is ever firm in three limbs (viz. the breast, waist and fist),
long in three (viz. the breast, waist and fist), long in three (viz.

the eyebrows, arms and soles), uniform in three (viz. his locks, testicles and knees), elevated in three (viz. his breast, rim of his navel and lower abdomen), coppery in three (viz. the rims of his eyes, nails, palms and soles), soft in three (viz. the lines on his soles, hair and the end of the membrane virile) and always deep in three (viz. the voice, gait and the navel).

Here is the third instance is used by Hanuman to describe the characteristics of Rama.

त्रिवलीवांस्त्र्यवनतश्चतुर्व्यङ्गस्त्रिशीर्षवान् ।
चतुष्कलश्चतुर्लेखश्चतुष्किष्कुश्चतुःसमः ।। (5–35–18)

He has three folds in the skin of his neck and belly. He is depressed at three places (viz. the middle of his soles, the lines on his soles and the nipples). He is undersized at four places (viz. the neck, membrane virile, the back and the shanks). He is endowed with three spirals in the hair of his head. He has four lines at the root of his thumb (denoting his proficiency in the four Vedas). He has four lines on his forehead (indicating longevity). He is four cubits high (96 inches). He has four pairs of limbs (viz. the cheeks, arms, shanks and knees) equally matched.

In the above shloka, the numbers 3 and 4 are used.

चतुष्कलः चतुः लेखः चतुष् किष्कुः चतुः समः ।
चतुर्दश सम द्वन्द्वः चतुः दष्टः चतुः गतिः ।। (5–35–19)

He has fourteen other pairs of limbs (viz. the eyebrows, nostrils, eyes, ears, lips, nipples, elbows, wrists, knees testicles, lions, hands, feet and thighs) equally matched. The four large teeth at both the ends of his upper and lower jaws are very sharp. He walks in four gaits (resembling the walks of a lion, a tiger, an elephant and a bull). He is endowed with excellent lips, chin and nose. He has five glossy limbs (viz. the hair, eyes, teeth, skin and soles). He has eight long limbs (viz. the arms, fingers and toes, eyes and ears, thighs and shanks).

दश पद्मो दश बृहत् त्रिभिः व्याप्तो दिव शुक्लवान्।
षड् उन्नतो नव तनुः त्रिभिः व्याप्नोति राघवः। (5–35–20)

Rama has ten lotus-like limbs (viz. the countenance, mouth, eyes, tongue, lips, palate, breasts, nails, hands and feet). He has ten ample limbs (viz. the chest, head, forehead, neck, arms, heart, mouth, feet, back and ears). He is spread through by reason of three (viz. splendor, renown and glory). He is doubly pure (on father's and mother's side). He is elevated in six limbs (viz. the flanks, abdomen, breast, nose, shoulders and the forehead). He is small, thin, fine or sharp in nine (viz. the hair, mustache and beard, nails the hair on the body, skin, finger-joints, the membrum virile, acumen and perception). He pursues religious merit, worldly riches and the sensuous delight in three periods (viz. the forenoon, midday and afternoon.) (Valmiki Ramayan Sarga 35, Sundar Kand)

In the above shloka, Hanuman has used the numbers 10, 3, 6 and 9.

There is another instance in the Ramayana where large numbers have been used to describe the strength of Rama's army. This instance is described in Udhya Kanda. Ravana, the king of Lanka abducted Sita, the wife of Rama, and held her captive in Ashok Vatika, Lanka. The great Hanuman searched for Sita and informed about her ill condition to Lord Rama who along with the Monkey King Sugriva, planned to attack Lanka to kill Ravana and set Sita free. They constructed 100 Yojana long and 10 Yojana wide bridge over the sea. When Rama reached Lanka along with his army, the Lanka King Ravana sent his spy Suka to know the strength of Rama's army; the spy Suka described the strength or Rama's army in the following manner.

शतं शत सहस्राणां कोटिमाहुर्मनीषिणः
शतं कोटिसहस्राणां शङ्कुरित्यभिधीयते ।। 6.28.33 ।।

शतं शङ्कुसहस्राणां महाशङ्कुरिति स्मृतः ।
महाशङ्कुंसहस्राणां शतं वृन्दमिहोच्यते ।। 6.28.34 ।।

शतं वृन्दसहस्राणां महावृन्दमिति स्मृतम् ।
महावृन्दसहस्राणां महापद्मिहोच्यते ।। 6.28.35 ।।

शतं पद्मसहस्राणां महापद्ममिति स्मृतम् ।
महापद्मसहस्राणां षतं खर्वमिहोच्यते ।। 6.28.36 ।।

शतं खर्वसहस्राणां महाखर्वमिति स्मृतम् ।
महाखर्वसहस्राणां समुद्रमभिधीयते ।। 6.28.37 ।।

शतं समुद्रसहस्रमोध इत्यभिधीयते ।
शतं मोधसहस्राणां महौध इति विश्रुतः ।। 6.28.38 ।।

(Valmikiya Ramayana, Yudhyakanda)

In simple words, the shloka mentioned above reveals that people in Treta Yuga have had knowledge of big numbers. Wise men call a hundred lakh as a crore. A hundred thousand crore is reckoned as a shanku. Let's write the meaning of shloka mathematically:

100 Lakh = 1 Koti = $10^7$

1 Lakh Koti = 1 Sanku = $10^{12}$

1 Lakh Sanku = 1 Mahasanku = $10^{17}$

1 Lakh Mahasanku = 1 Vrinda = $10^{22}$

1 Lakh Vrinda = 1 Maha Vrinda = $10^{27}$

1 Lakh Maha Vrinda = 1 Padma = $10^{32}$

1 Lakh Padma = 1 Maha Padma = $10^{37}$

1 Lakh Maha Padma = 1 Kharava = $10^{42}$

1 Lakh Kharva = 1 Maha Kharva = $10^{47}$

1000 Mahakharva = 1 Samudra = $10^{50}$

1 Lakh Samudra = 1 Auogh = $10^{55}$

1 Lakh Auogh = 1 Mahaaugh = $10^{60}$

If you add up all the above numbers, you will get a very large number which is out of our imagination and the best part is that these numbers in the multiple of 10 were known to people during Treta Yuga period.

एषाम् कोटि सहस्राणि नव पन्च च सप्त च ।
तथा शन्ख सहस्राणि तथा वृन्द शतानि च ।। 6—28—4

(There are twenty-one thousand crore, a thousand Shankus and a hundred Vrindas of these monkeys. 1 hundred lakhs = 1 crore and 1 hundred thousand crores = 1 shanku.)

S.S.N. Murthy, in his article, writes that there are several instances in Ramayana which show the importance of number 10:

(a) The number of heads of Ravana is 10.
(b) The battle between Rama and Ravana lasts for 10 days
(c) The number of years Rama spends in the forest of Dandaka is 10.
(d) Rama had performed 10 Asvamedha yagans.
(e) The reference to 10 directions is also evident at many places in Ramayana.

This shows that the importance of number in multiples of 10 is prevalent in our religious texts.

## Numbers in the Mahabharata

The Mahabharata is one of the major Sanskrit epics of ancient India written by Maharshi Ved Vyas. It contains much philosophical and devotional material including the four goals of life called purushartha. It is the longest Sanskrit epic. It's longest version contains over 100,000 shlokas and around 1.8 million words in total. The number 18 keeps coming in the Mahabharata. The epic has been divided into 18 sections or parvas. These parvas are:

1. Aathiparvam
2. Sabhaparvam

10. Sowmthigaparvam
11. Shreeparvam

3. Vanaparvam
4. Viradaparvam
5. Udyogaparvam
6. Bheshmaparvam
7. Droonaparvam
8. Karnaparvam
9. Saalyaparvam

12. Shanthiparvam
13. Anusasanaparvam
14. Ashvamedaparvam
15. Aashramparvam
16. Mowsalaparvam
17. Mahprasthanikaparvam
18. Swarkahoranaparvam

*Manuscript illustration of Battle of Kurukshetera in the Mahabharata*
*(Source: http://www.atributetohinduism.com/Hindu_Scriptures.htm)*

These 18 parvas deals with a battle that was fought over 18 days and involved 18 Akshauhini armies (11 Akshauhini to Kaurava and 7 Akshauhini to Pandavas). Yudhishitra lost all his wealth in the 18th game of gamble. The revered book Bhagavad Gita, which is part of the Mahabharata, has 18 chapters in all.

The description of the armies as found in the Mahabharata is in numbers—1, 2, 3, 4, 7, 10, 11, 18, 100, 1000, and the bigger number like hundreds of crore.

चतुर्युजो रथाः सर्वे सर्वे चोत्तम वाजिनः।
सप्रास ऋष्टिकाः सर्वे सर्वे शतशरासनाः।।
रथस्यासन् दश गजा गजस्य दश वाजिनः।
नरा दश हयस्यासन् पादरक्षाः समन्ततः।।
सेना पंचशतं नागा रथास्तावन्त एव च।
दश सेना च पूतना पूतना दशवाहिनी।।

The above shloka describes that there were 4 horses tied to each chariot and 100 bows were kept on each chariot. Ten elephants were following a chariot and 10 horses followed an elephant. Ten foot soldiers were following a horse. It means a chariot was being followed by $10 \times 10 \times 10 = 1,000$ armies. This is not all, a sena consisted of 500 elephants and 500 chariots.

10 sena = 1 putana and

10 Putana = 1 vahini

Hence, 1 Vahini = 100 sena

1 sena = 500 elephants + 500 chariots

1 chariot = 1000 armies

Hence, 500 chariots = $500 \times 1000 = 5,00,000$ armies.

In the Mahabharata, Akshauhini is the term described for Chaturanga sena. The sena used to have four major parts of the armychariots, elephants, horses and soldiers in it.

One Akshauhini sena had 21,870 chariots, 21,870 elephants, 65,610 horses and 109,350 foot soldiers. Interestingly, these numbers are in the ratio of 1: 1: 3: 5. Assuming two people stood on a chariot and two people rode an elephant the approximate calculation is: $2 \times 21870 + 2 \times 21870 + 65610 + 109350 = 2,62,440$ fighter per Akshauhini.

अक्षौहिण्यस्तु सप्तैव पाण्डवानाम भूद्बलम।
अक्षौहिण्यो दशकै च कौरवणाय भूद्बलम।।

There were 7 Akshauhini senas with Pandavas and 11 Akshauhini senas with Kauravas making the total number of soldiers in 18 Akshauhini = 18 × 262440 = 4723920 men. This is a very large number of soldiers fighting a battle, isn't it? This too shows that people during Treta Yuga when the Mahabharata was fought was well versed in using large numbers.

In Stri Parva of the Mahabharata, there is an instance after the Kuruskshetra War, the Pandavas along with Krishna meet Dhrithrasta and Gandhari in Hastinapur. Dhrithrastra asked Yudhisthira if he had a count of people who died and survived. Yudhistra replied:

दशायुतानाम अयुतं सहस्राणि च विंशतिः।
कोट्यः षष्टिश च षट चैव ये ऽस्मिन राजमृधे हताः।।
अलक्ष्याणां तु वीराणां सहस्राणि चतुर्दश।
दश चान्यानि राजेन्द्र शतं षष्टिश च पञ्च च।।

(Mathematically, the fatalities = 1 billion, 660 million, 20,000 = 1000,000,000 + 660,000,000 + 20,000 = 1660,020,000

Survivors = 240165)

The Mahabharata also describes the age of person in different yugas. Sanjay describes the age of person in Satya Yuga, Treta Yuga, Dwapar Yuga and Kali Yuga:

चत्वारि भारते वर्षे युगानि भरतवर्शम्
कृतं त्रेता द्वापरं च तिष्टां च कुरूवर्धनम्।।

चत्वारि तु सहस्राणि वर्षाने कुरूसप्तम।
आयुः संस्था कृतयुगे संख्याता राजसप्तम।।
तथा त्रीणि सहस्राणि त्रेतायां मनुजाधिप।
द्वे सहस्रे द्वापरे तु मुनि तिष्ठति साम्प्रताम।।

The above shloka speaks that the age of a person in a particular yuga is as follows:

Sata Yuga = 4000 years

Treat Yuga = 3000 years

Dwapar Yuga = 2000 years

Among the principal narratives of the Mahabharata is the story of King Nala and his wife Damayanti. The story begins when King Nala loses everything, including his kingdom, in a dice game. He abandons his faithful and loving wife, Damayanti, for her own good. After a series of misadventures, Damayanti is reunited with her parents and their two children. Meanwhile Nala, under the assumed name of Vahuka, obtains a position as the cook and charioteer of the King of the Forest, Rituparna. Under King Rituparna, Nala learns the art of dice playing. Meanwhile, Damayanti devises an ingenious plan for bringing Rituparna, and therefore his driver, Nala, to her father's castle. A 'mathematical incident', which involved playing Chaushar or game of dice to check the skill of number, occurs on the way, after which Nala arrives free of the passion for gambling and they live happily ever after.

In this story, the concepts of probability and gambling appear in Mahabharata. The King Rituparna was a master of gambling. He once said:

विद्यक्षहृदयज्ञं मां सङ्ख्याने च विशारदं

(Knowledge I possess of the game of dice, this is my skill in number.)

According to Nalopakhyanam, King Rituparna estimated accurately the number of leaves of a tree to be panchkoti (50 billion).

वृक्षेऽस्मिन् यानि पर्णानि फलान्यापि च वाहक ।
पतितान्यापि यान्यच तवैकम् अधिकं शतं ।। 9 ।।
एकम् अवाधिकं पचं फलम् एकं च वाहक।
पंचकोट्योऽथ पचानां हयोर् अपि च शाखयो: ।।10।।
प्रचिनुह्यस्य शाखे द्वे याश्चाप्यन्या: प्रशाखिका: ।
आभ्यां फलसहस्रे द्वे पंचोनं शतम् एव च ।।11।।

After the disappearance of King Nala, his wife Damayanti and his father in law sent courtiers to different places to search King Nala. Someone told queen Damayanti that King Nala was seen in Ayodhya. To test the fact it was proclaimed that queen has assented to remarry and consequently an invitation was sent to Rituparna's court where Nala was working. Nala was the best chariot driver so he offered his service to Rituparna and with his magical art they reached the palace in seconds. Nala taught Rituaparna the secret techniques of fast chariot driving. In the way while passing through a forest the King Rituparna enquired Nala whether he could count the leaves of tree and Nala then counted the number of leaves. He began to say that the leaves and fruits fallen down are 2 more than 100. The number of leaves of two branches of tree is 5 crore and the number of fruits in this tree counts to 2095.

There are several such instances in the Mahabharata where you can find big numbers used during those days by the people. I would lastly love to put a large number in front of my avid reader.

In Bhumi Parva of the Mahabharata, the area of Jambudwip has been described with the following shlokas:

अष्टादश सहस्राणि योजनानि विशाम्पते ।
षट् शतानि च पूर्णानि विष्कंभो जम्बु पर्वत: ।।

According to this shloka, the area of Jambudwip is 18,600 yojana = 238,080 km. Though this area is not equal to the area of India in the present context but, it is worth noting that people at that time were also keen to find the area of the country.

## Number in the Hanuman Chalisa

The Hanuman Chalisa is one of the most revered books of Hindu religion which describes Hanuman as the avatar of Shankara and his magnificent power. This book is written by Goswami Tulsidas and is written in couplets. There is an instance where the distance between the sun and the earth is discussed.

युग सहस्त्र योजन पर भानू ।
लील्यो ताहि मधुर फल जानू ।।

Here is the mathematical explanation which described the distance of the sun and the earth.

1 Yuga (युग) = 12,000 years

1 Shahastra (सहस्त्र) = 1,000

1 Yojana (योजन) = 8 mile

Hence, yuga Shahastra yojana (युग सहस्त्र योजन) = 12,000 × 1,000 × 8 mile = 96,000,000 mile

1 mile = 1.6 km

96000000 = 1.6 × 96,000,000 = 1536,000,000 km

There is another couplet in the Hanuman Chalisa that tells about the supernatural power of the gods:

अष्ट सिद्धि नव निधि के दाता
अस वर दिन्ह जानकी माता

(Goddess Sita has granted you the boon to become a bestower of eight supernatural powers and nine divine treasures.)

The eight siddhis (supernatural powers) are:

1. Aṇimā: Ability to reduce one's size
2. Mahima: Ability to increase one's size
3. Garima: Ability to increase one's weight infinitely
4. Laghima: Ability to become lighter than the lightest
5. Prāpti: Ability to obtain anything
6. Prākāmya: Ability to acquire anything desired
7. Iṣiṭva: Lordship over creation
8. Vaśitva: Having control over things

The nine nidhis (treasures) are:

1. Mahapadma: Great lotus flower
2. Padma: Lotus/ a Himalayan lake with treasures
3. Shankha: Conch shell
4. Makara: Crocodile/ Antimony
5. Kachchhapa: Tortoise or turtle shell
6. Mukunda: Cinnabar/ Quick Silver
7. Kunda: Jasmine/ Arsenic
8. Nila: Sapphire/ Antimony
9. Kharva: Cups, vessels baked in fire

Moreover in the Surya Siddhanta, the measurement of angles is identical to the present system.

विकलानां कलाबस्टयाः तत् षस्टया भाग उच्यते
तत्रिंशतां भवेद्राशिः भगणो द्वादशैव ते।

In modern notation, Vikala is a second, Kala is a minute and Bhaga is a degree.

According to this:

60 Vikala = 1 Kala

60 Kala = 1 Bhaga

30 Bhaga = 1 Rashi

12 Rashi = 1 Bhagana

## Number in Durga Saptashati

The Sri Durga Saptashati contains 700 shlokas (sapta=7, shata=100 verses) depicting Hindu Goddess Durga. This count includes one-line sentences which are not strictly verses. There is another opinion that the name should be Saptashati, as it deals with the story of seven Satis or 'pious persons'. The seven mothers are Brahmi, Maheshwari, Kaumari, Vaisnhnavi, Varahi, Indrani and Chamunda.

This book has thirteen chapters divided into three episodes that depict the battle of Goddess Durga with various demons. The most famous battle described in this book is the battle with Mahishasura (buffalo demon).

This book describes the victory of Goddess Durga over Mahishasura. It was composed in Sanskrit around 400–500 BC by Rishi Markandeya, who is known to have defeated the Death God Yama due to his worship of Lord Shiva.

The *Devī Māhātmya* (Discourses on Devi Durga) consists of chapters 81–93 of the Mārkandeya Purana, one of the early Sanskrit Puranas, which is a set of stories being narrated by Sage Markandeya to Jaimini and his students (who are in the form of birds).

As far as this book is concerned, numbers in billion and trillion are described in many shlokas. Even the smallest number 1, 2, 3, 7, 9, 32 and 108 has been used in many places. Besides that 1,000, 100,000, 1,000,000 and numbers in crore in many chapters have taken places. Let's begin our journey to trace the instances where these numbers have been used.

This book begins with seven sholkas (सप्त श्लोकी) and two of them have been discussed here describing the numbers 3 and 4.

सर्वमंगलमांगल्ये शिवे सर्वार्थसाधिके ।
शरण्ये त्र्यम्बके गौरी नारायणि नमोऽस्तु ते ।।

(You are the Auspiciousness in All the Auspicious, Auspiciousness Yourself, Complete with All the Auspicious Attributes, and You fulfill All the Objectives of the Devotees (Purusharthas (पुरुषार्थ)— Dharma (धर्म), Artha (अर्थ), Kama (काम) and Moksha (मोक्ष)), You are the Giver of Refuge, You have Three Eyes (spanning the Past, Present and Future; and containing within them the Sun, Moon and the Fire), You are Gauri (the Shining One); Salutations to You, O Narayani.)

सर्वाबाधाप्रशमनं त्रैलोक्यस्याखिलेश्वरि ।।
एवमेव त्वया कार्यमस्मद्वैरि विनाशनम् ।।

(Salutations to You, O Jagadamba, O Goddess of All the Three Worlds (1. Svargaok, स्वर्गलोक 2. Martya Lok मृत्युलोक and 3. Pātāla Lok पाताललोक), when You are Pleased, You Mitigate All Our Distresses. Thus, in this Manner, Your Grace Works to Destroy our Inner Enemies.)

This book talks about 108 names of Goddess Durga and talks that jaaps or dhyana of 108 names may please her.

ॐ सती साध्वी भवप्रीता भवानी भवमोचिनी ।
आर्या दुर्गा जया चाद्या त्रिनेत्रा शूलधारिणी ।।
शिवदूती कराली च अनन्ता परमेश्वरी ।
कात्यायनी च सावित्री प्रत्यक्षा ब्रह्मवादिनी ।।15।।
य इदं प्रपठेन्नित्यं दुर्गानामशताष्टकम्
नासाध्यं विद्यते देवि त्रिषु लोकेषु पार्वति ।।16।।

The above shlokas with 16 stanzas describe the 108 names of Goddess Durga and reveal the importance of reciting these 108 names. This book talks that one who recites the 108 names of Goddess Durga daily can achieve everything in the entire universe, that is, in all three world.

During the Durga Puja, a festival celebrated for 9 days during which the devotees worship the 9 faces (रूप) of Goddess Durga. According to Hindu mythology, these 9 faces are the manifestation of Parvati. These 9 faces of Durga are—ShailaPutri (शैलपुत्री), Brahmachārinī (ब्रह्मचारिणी), Chandraghantā (चंद्रघंटा), Kushmāndā (कुष्मांडा), Skandamātā (स्कंदमाता), Kārtyāyanī (कात्यायनी), Kālarātrī (कालरात्रि), Mahāgaurī (महागौरी) and Siddhidātrī (सिद्धिदात्री).

प्रथम शैलपुत्री च द्वितीय ब्रह्मचारिणी।
तृतीयं चंद्रघण्टेति कूष्मांडेति चतुर्थकम्।।
पंचमं स्कन्दमातेति षष्ठं कात्यायनीति च।

सप्तमं कालरात्रीति महागौरीति चाष्टम् ।।
नवमं सिद्धिदात्री च नवदुर्गाः प्रकीर्तिताः ।
उक्तान्येतानि नामानि ब्रह्मणैव महात्मना ।।

In chapter 2, the numbers thousand, sixty lakhs, one crore and five billion are used.

दिशो भुजसहस्रेण समन्ताद् व्याप्य संस्थिताम् ।
ततः प्रववृते युद्धं तया देव्या सुरद्विषाम् ।।2.39।।
शस्त्रास्त्रैर्बहुधा मुक्तैरादीपितदिगन्तरम्
महिषासुरसेनारीशिचक्षुराख्यो महासुरः ।।2.40।।
अयुध्यतायुतानां च सहस्रेण महाहनुः ।
अयुतानां शतैः षड्भिर्बाष्कलो युयुधे रणे ।
गजवाजिसहस्रौघैरनेकैः परिवारितः ।।2.43।।
वृतो रथानो कोट्या च युद्धे तस्मिन्नयुध्यत ।
बिडालाख्योऽयुतानां च पंचाशद्भिरथायुतैः ।।2.44।।
युयुधे संयुगे तत्र रथानां परिवारितः ।
अन्ये च तत्रायुतशे रथनागहयैर्वृताः ।।2.45।।
युयुधुः संयुगं देव्या सह तत्र महासुरः ।
कोटिकोटिसहस्रैस्तु सस्तु रथानां दन्तिनां तथा ।।2.46।।

The number 1,000 (सहस्र), 10,000 (अयुत), 10,000,000 (कोटि), are used in the above shloka.

1 अयुत = 10,000     1 शतः = 100     षड् = 6
अयुतानां शतैः षड = 6 × 100 × 10,000 = 6000,000 = 60 lac

Making the earth bend with her footstep, scraping the sky with her diadem, shaking the netherworld with the twang of the bowstring, and standing there pervading all the quarters around with *her thousand arms*. Then began a battle between that Devi and the enemies of the devas, in which the quarters of the sky were illumined by the weapons and arms hurled diversely. Mahisasura's general, a great asura named Ciksura and Camara, attended by forces comprising four parts, and others (asuras) fought. A great asura named Udagra with *sixty thousand chariots*, and Mahahanu with *ten million* (of chariots) gave battle. Asiloman, another great asura, with *fifteen million* (of chariots), and Baskala with *six million* fought in that battle. Privarita with many thousands of elephants and horses, and surrounded by *ten million of chariots*, fought in that battle. An asura named Bidala fought in that battle surrounded with *five hundred crores* of chariots. And other great asuras, thousands in number, surrounded with chariots, elephants and horses fought with the Devi in that battle. Mahisasura was surrounded in that battle with *thousands of crore* of horses, elephants and chariots. Others (asuras) fought in the battle with iron maces and javelins, spears, clubs, swords, axes and halberds. Some hurled spears and others nooses.

There is another shloka in chapter 1 that speaks about the number 5,000. This shloka says that Shri Hari fought with demons Madhu and Kaitava for 5,000 years.

पंचवर्ष सहस्राणि बाहुप्रहरणो विभुः
तावप्याति बलोन्मत्तौ महामायाविमोहितौ ।९४।

The above information proves that mathematics can be found in many Hindu scriptures. The Shiv sashra naam shlokas sung during the Mahabharata war tells the 1,000 names of God Shankar.

## Importance of Nine

Nine is the highest one digit number with a special place in the Hindu tradition. The Bhagavatpurana mentions nine forms of devotion—Sravanam (Hearing about God), Kirtanam (singing the praise of God), Mananam (remembering God), Padaseva (serving the feet of God), Archanam (Worshiping God), Mantram (offering prayer to God), Seva (Seving the cause of God), Maitri (friendship with God) and Saranam (Surrender to God).

Lord Kubera, the god of wealth, is described as the possessor of nine nidhis.

In a naulakha necklace, we find the reference of nine precious stones namely—मुक्ता (Mukta), माणिक (Manikya), वैदूर्य (Vaidhurya), गोमेद (Gomedhika), हीरा (Diamond), पदमराग (Padmaraga), मूंगा (Munga), पन्ना (Marakantana) and नीलम (Nilam) which are probably related in some way to the nine treasures of Kubera.

The 'Fruit of the Spirit' comprises nine graces: love, peace, suffering, gentle, good, faith, meek and temperance. There are 'gifts of the Spirit' nine: the word of wisdom, the word of knowledge, faith, healing, miracles, prophecy, discerning of spirits, tongues, and interpretation of tongues.

The Durga has nine of manifestations.

There are nine rasas which are the essential aspects or enegies that define a set of emotions and moods—Shringara, Hasya, Adbhuta, Shanta, Raudra, Veera, Karuna, Bhayanaka and Vibhatsa.

## Number in the Holy Quran

The Quran is believed to be a revelation from God. It is considered to be the only book that has been protected by God from distortion.

*96th Sura of the Quran—the first revelation received by Muhammad*
*(Source: Marvels of Number Seven in the Noble Quran*
*by Abdul Daem Al Kaheel)*

It is my candid admission to all readers that I have not studied the Quran in its original format but during my research. I found a book *The Marvels of the Number Seven in the Noble Qur'an* written by Abdul Daem Al Kaheel and translated by Mohammed R. Al Salah. It is very interesting and as references to the number in the Quran. Besides that, I found some articles written by Rashid Khalifa, highlighting the numbers in the Quran. I am highly indebted to these two men for placing information of Holy Quran in mathematical context in a beautiful manner and the content in the following paragraphs are attributed to them. I have only cited references to numbers in the Quran as that is the focal point of this book.

1.  The first page of the Holy Quran has the following verse.

    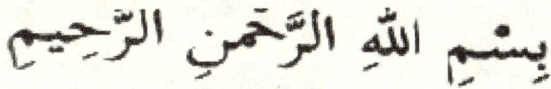

    [In the name of GOD, Most Gracious, Most Merciful (Al-Fatihah, 1:1).] This verse carries an astonishing numeric fact because when you count its letters just as they appear in the Quran, you will find it consists of exactly 19 letters.
2.  The first verse of Surat an-Nasr, which speaks of the help of Allah, contains 19 letters.

    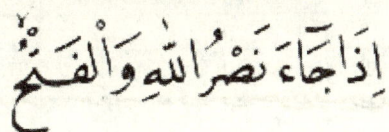

| | | | | | |
|---|---|---|---|---|---|
| ا | 1st letter | ص | 8th letter | ا | 15th letter |
| ذ | 2nd letter | ر | 9th letter | ل | 16th letter |
| ا | 3rd letter | ا | 10th letter | ف | 17th letter |

| | | | | | |
|---|---|---|---|---|---|
| جَ | 4th letter | ا | 11th letter | بْ | 18th letter |
| ا | 5th letter | ل | 12th letter | ح | 19th letter |
| ء | 6th letter | ه | 13th letter | | |
| نْ | 7th letter | و | 14th letter | | |

3. The Quran consists of 114 suras, which is 6 times 19.

$$114 = 19 \times 6$$

4. There are 6234 numbered verses and 112 un-numbered verses in the holy Quran and its total comes out to be 6346 (6234 + 112 = 6346). The digit sum of 6346 is again 19.

$$6 + 3 + 4 + 6 = 19.$$

The interesting part of this number is that it is also the multiple of 19.

$$6346 = 19 \times 334$$

5. The word 'Allah' (God) occurs in the Quran 2698 times which is again the multiple of 19.

$$2698 = 19 \times 142$$

6. In the Holy Quran, 30 different numbers are mentioned. They are:

| | | | | |
|---|---|---|---|---|
| 1 | 7 | 19 | 70 | 1.000 |
| 2 | 8 | 20 | 80 | 2.000 |
| 3 | 9 | 30 | 99 | 3.000 |
| 4 | 10 | 40 | 100 | 5.000 |
| 5 | 11 | 50 | 200 | 50.000 |
| 6 | 12 | 60 | 300 | 100.000 |

More interestingly, the sum of these numbers is 162146 which is once again the multiple of 19.

$$162146 = 19 \times 8534$$

7. The Holy Quran also talks about fractional numbers.

There are reference of numbers like 1/10, 1/8, 1/6, 1/5, 1/4, 1/3, 1/2 and 2/3.

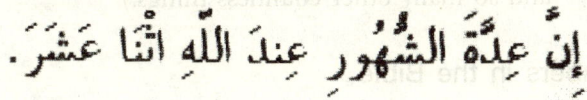

*(Source: Quran and Mathematics by Noor Muhammad Awan)*

[They ask thee for a legal decision. Say: Allah directs (thus) about those who leave no descendants or ascendants as heirs. If it is a man that dies, leaving a sister but no child, she shall have half the inheritance: If (such a deceased was) a woman, who left no child, Her brother takes her inheritance: If there are two sisters, they shall have two-thirds of the inheritance (between them): if there are brothers and sisters, (they share), the male having twice the share of the female. Thus doth Allah make clear to you (His law), lest ye err. And Allah hath knowledge of all things.]

8. In the holy Quran, the word 'month' appears 12 times and we know that there are exactly 12 months in a year.

إِنَّ عِدَّةَ الشُّهُورِ عِنْدَ اللَّهِ اثْنَا عَشَرَ.

(The number of months in the sight of Allah is 12)

9. The word 'day' appears in the Quran 365 times. As you all are aware of the fact that there are 365 days in a normal year.

10. The word 'sea' appears 32 times and 'land' appears 13 times in the Quran. Dr Tariq Al Swaidan explains that the sum of digits thus comes out to be 32 + 13 = 45.

Now the mathematical part of this reference can be seen as:

% of SEA = 32/ 45 × 100 = 71.111…

% of LAND = 13/ 45 × 100 = 28.888…

Modern science has proved the above figures are correct.

11. The number 7 comes many a time in the Quran.

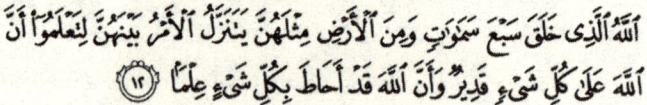

It is Allah who has created seven heavens and of the earth the like. His command descends between them, that you may know that Allah has power over all things, and that Allah surrounds all things in (His) knowledge. (Al-Talaq 65:12).

(The number 7 has a great presence in our life and worship because the heavens are 7, the colours are 7, the days are 7, the orbits in an atom are 7, we turn around the Kaaba 7 times, we run between Safa and Marwa 7 times, we stone Lucifer 7 times, we are commanded by 7 commands, we are forbidden to commit 7 sins, the greatest sins that directly lead to Hell are 7, there are 7 kinds of people Allah will put them under His shade on the day of judgment, and so many other countless things.)

## Numbers in the Bible

The Bible is a sacred epic of Judaism as well as in Christianity. It is my candid admission that I have not gone through the Bible to find such information. I have based all my arguments on the book I have gone through and websites I have come across. This is purely an informative section and does intend to hurt the sentiments of any religious people.

The number 1 has been used throughout the Bible to indicate one thing only, God Himself: 'Thou shalt have no other gods besides me.'

The number 3 is often thought to be the number of divine perfection in the Bible, such as the Trinity consisting of the Father, the Son and the Holy Spirit. The number 3 is first introduced in the beginning of God's creation as His introductory face— Evening, Morning and Day.

The numbers 1, 2, 3, 4, 5, 6, 7, 8, 9, 10, 11, 12, 13, 14, 15, 16, 17, 20, 30, 40, 42, 50, 70, 120, 153, etc. have been discussed in many occasions in the Bible.

There are some instances that show that pi ($\pi$) has been used in the Bible.

And he [Hiram] made a molten sea, ten cubits from the one rim to the other it was round all about and... a line of thirty cubits did compass it round about... And it was an hand breadth thick—First King, chapter 7, verses 23 and 26.

The Molten Sea
(Source: http://3.bp.blogspot.com/-BWViyAdslAw/U_9nCopdaYI/
AAAAAAAAQxk/tyy8n4SZWN4/s1600/MJ%2B2014%2Bbrasen%2BSea%2B1.jpg)

The bowl (see the figure below) is said to have had a circumference of 30 cubits and a diameter of 10 cubits. The diameter is said to be 'from one rim to the other', so this would be the outer diameter; that is; the diameter of the outer mold used to make the bowl.

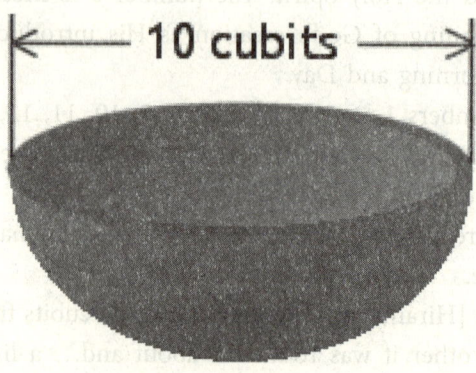

Hence, π = 30/ 10 = 3

People also used mathematics to build King Solomon's Pool. It was 10 cubits in distance, 5 in height and its circumference or distance around was 30 cubits. Priests used this pool to bathe before entering into a holy place. It is evident that the architect who was responsible for making the pool had to have had some knowledge of pi.

The number 6 is another important number that appears in the Bible. Saint Augustine in the Old Testament writes that although God could have created the world all at once, he preferred to take 6 days. The number 6 is often considered to be the number of man in the Bible, since man was created on the 6th day by God.

There are many instances where number 7 has been used in Bible. The number 7 permeates the totality of scripture because it speaks of God's divine perfection and perfect order. It is considered to be 'God's number', since He is the only one who is perfect and complete. God could have created the world all at once, but he took 6 days to complete the universe and kept the 7th day for rest. On the first day God created light. This was number 1. On the second day God separated the firmament from the water. Thus the characteristics of the number 2 is division or separation. On the third day, God set the heavens in the proper relationship to planet earth. This included the sun, moon, Solar system, the stars and all other heavenly bodies. Thus 4 represents the relationship of the earth to heavens. On the fifth day, God created the animal kingdom. On the sixth day, God made man. On the seventh day God rested.

In Revelation God is said to have 7 Spirits, depicted as 7 lamp stands. There are 31,102 verses in the King James Bible and when you add the sum of its digits (3 + 1 + 1 + 0 + 2), you will get 7.

W.E. Filmer in a wonderful booklet called *God Counts* has depicted the beautiful association with numbers in the Bible.

ברא שית ברא אלהים את השמים ואת הארץ

| 200 | 5 400 | 8 40 | 5 400 1 40 | 1 1 | 2 400 | 5 |

| EARTH | AND THE | HEAVENS | THE | GOD | CRE-ATED | IN THE BEGINNING |

*Numbers in the Bible (Source: God Counts by W.E. Filmer)*

The Genesis 1:1 of The Old Testament reads: 'In the beginning God created the heavens and the earth.' The original sentence in Hebrew contains 7 words and 28 letters (7 × 4). The sentence is divided into two equal parts: the first three words—in the beginning God created, contains 14 letters (2 × 7) and the other four words—the heavens and the earth contain 14 letters (2 × 7). The three nouns—God, heavens and earth—have all together 14 letters (2 × 7). The numeric value of these three nouns is 777 which is again the multiple of multiple of 7

$$777 = 7 \times 111.$$

The Holy Bible has also given description about 666, which is known to be the Beast's number. In the Revelation 13.18, the Bible says: 'Here is wisdom. Let him that hath understanding count the number of the beast: for it is the number of a man; and his number is Six hundred three score and six.'

In another instance, the Bible says:

'Now the weight of gold that came to Solomon in one year was six hundred threescore and six talents of gold.'

Even the Bible talks about big numbers like in Chapter 1, verse 21:

'But Moses said, "people, among whom I am, are 600,000 on foot"; yet you have said, "I will give them meat, so that they may eat for a whole month".'

The King James Bible even talks about mathematical terms like area, length, breadth and height.

The house that King Solomon built for the Lord was 60 cubits long, 20 cubits wide and 30 cubits high. The vestibule in front of the nave of the house was 20 cubits long, equal to the width of the house and 10 cubits deep in front of the house. (King 6 : 2-3)

Here the dimension of the house is discussed in the Bible. The point to remember is that 1 cubit = 18 inches or 45 centimetres.

The Genesis 6: 15–16 also explains the dimension of the house to be built in numbers like 300, 50 and 30.

This is how you are to make it: the length of the ark 300 cubits, its breadth 50 cubits and its height 30 cubits. Make a roof for the ark, and finish it to a cubit above, and set the door of the ark in its side. Make it with lower, second and third decks.

## Numbers and Buddhism

Since the time of the Vedas, large numbers are in use. The epics of Hindu religion—the Vedas, the Ramayana, the Mahabharata and so on—talk about large numbers as described above. The Buddhism followed the footprint of Hinduism and talked about much larger number. The great writer of *History of Mathematics*, F. Cajori says, 'At the early period the Hindus exhibited great skill in calculating, even with large numbers. Thus, they tell us of an examination to which Buddha, the reformer of the Indian religion, had to submit, when a youth in order to win the maiden he loved. In arithmetic, after having astonished his examiners by naming all the periods of number up to $53^{rd}$, he was asked whether he could determine the number of primary atoms which, when placed one against the other, would form a line one mile in length. Buddha found the required answer in that way:—7 primary atoms make a very minute grain of dust, 7 of these a grain of dust whirled up by the wind and so on. Thus he proceeded, step-by-step, until he finally reached the length of a mile. The multiplication of all the factors gave for the multitude of primary atoms in a mile a number consisting of 15 digits.'

*(Source: Lalitvistara, Published by The Asiatic Society [2001])*

A book *Lalitvitsara* (circa 100 BC), which tells the story of Buddha's life talks about numbers up to $10^{53}$. According to this book, King Suddodhana wanted a beautiful girl with all qualities for his son, Prince Gautam (who later became Gautam Buddha), and Princess Gopa was considered fit for him. In the swayamvara, Prince Gautam competed with five other suitors for the hand of Gopa the daughter of King Dandapani. Gautam defeated all in writing, wrestling, archery, running and swimming and a number of skills. He was called for the final test by mathematician Arjuna who asked, 'O, young man, do you know the counting which goes beyond the koti on the centesimal scale?'

And Viswamitra said, "It is enough, Let us to numbers.
After me repeat
Your numeration till we reach the Lakh,
One, two, three, four, to ten, and then by tens
To hundreds, thousands." After him the child

Named digits, decades, centuries; nor paused,
The round lakh reached, but softly murmured on
"Then comes the kôti, nahut, ninnahut,
Khamba, viskhamba, abab, attata,
To kumuds, gundhikas, and utpalas,
By pundarîkas unto padumas,
Which last is how you count the utmost grains
Of Hastagiri ground to finest dust;
But beyond that a numeration is,
The Kâtha, used to count the stars of night;
The Kôti-Kâtha, for the ocean drops;
Ingga, the calculus of circulars;
Sarvanikchepa, by the you deal
With all the sands of Ganga, till we come
To Antah-Kalpas, where the unit is
The sands of ten crore Ganga. If one seeks
More comprehensive scale, th' arithmetic mounts
By the Asankya, which is the tale
Of all the drops that in ten thousand years
Would fall on all the worlds by daily rain;
Thence unto Maha Kalpas, by the which
The Gods compute their future and their past.
"'Tis good," the Sage rejoined, "Most noble Prince,
If these thou know'st, needs it that I should teach
The mensuration of the lineal?"
Humbly the boy replied, "Acharya!"
"Be pleased to hear me. Paramânus ten
A parasukshma make; ten of those build
The trasarene, and seven trasarenes
One mote's-length floating in the beam, seven motes
The whisker-point of mouse, and ten of these
One likhya; likhyas ten a yuka, ten

Yukas a heart of barley, which is held
Seven times a wasp-waist; so unto the grain
Of mung and mustard and the barley-corn,
Whereof ten give the finger-joint, twelve joints
The span, wherefrom we reach the cubit, staff,
Bow-length, lance-length; while twenty lengths of lance
Mete what is named a 'breath, which is to say
Such space as man may stride with lungs once filled,
Whereof a gow is forty, four times that
A yôjana; and, Master! if it please,
I shall recite how many sun-motes lie
From end to end within a yôjana."
Thereat, with instant skill, the little Prince
Pronounced the total of the atoms true.

(Source: 'Book the First', *The Light of Asia: Or, the Great Renunciation* by Edwin Arnold)

Buddha's response was: 'Hundred kotis are called ayuta, hundred ayutas are called niyuta, hundred niyutas are called kankara—and continued to tallaksana which is $10^{53}$.'

| 100 Koti = 1 Ayuta | 100 Ayuta = 1 Niyuta |
|---|---|
| 100 Niyuta = 1 Kankar | 100 Kankar = 1 Vivar |
| 100 Vivar = 1 Akshobhya | 100 Akshobhya = 1 Vivah |
| 100 Vivah = 1 Utsang | 100 Utsang = 1 Bahul |
| 100 Bahul = 1 Nagabal | 100 Nagabal = 1 Titilambh |
| 100 Titilambh = 1 Vyavasthan Pragyapati | 100 Vyavasthan Pragyapati = 1 Hetuhil |
| 100 Hetuhil = 1 Karku | 100 Karku = 1 Hetvindriya |
| 100 Hetvindriya = 1 Samaptalambh | 100 Samaptalambh = 1 Gannagati |
| 100 Gannagati = 1 Nirbadhya | 100 Nirbadhya = 1 Mudrabal |

| 100 Mudrabal = 1 Sarvabal | 100 Sarvabal = 1 Vishangyagati |
|---|---|
| 100 Vishangyagati = 1 Sarvasangya | 100 Sarvasangya = 1 Vibhutangma |
| 100 Vibhutangma = 1 Tallaksana. | |

With the help of numeration called tallaksana, one could take even Meru, the king of Mountains, as a subject of calculation and measure it. That is not the end of the story. Later Buddha continued with 8 more counts (Dyajafravati, Dvajagranisamani, Vahanaprajnapti, Inga, Kuruta, Sarvaniskspa, Agrasara and Uttaraparamanurajahpravesa). He counted for 23 numbers in succession in the base of 100 as shown in tables and the 23rd number was called Tallaksana which is $100^{23}$ kotis or $10^{53}$. Later he added 8 more numbers which in numerical values equal to $10^{421}$.

The highest number discovered by modern mathematicians is Googolplex which is equal to $10^{googol}$.

Buddhism talks about much larger numbers. 'Bukeshuo bukeshuo zhuan' is one of them. It is $10^{37218383881977644441306597687849648128}$ which appeared as Bodhisattva's maths in the Avatamsaka Sutra.

Following are a few large numbers used in India in about fifth century BC (*See Georges Ifrah: A Universal History of Numbers,* pp. 422–423):

- *lakṣá* (लक्ष) —$10^5$
- *kōti* (कोटि) —$10^7$
- *ayuta* (अयुत) —$10^9$
- *niyuta* (नियुत) —$10^{13}$
- *pakoti* (पकोटि) —$10^{14}$
- *vivara* (विवारा) —$10^{15}$
- *kshobhya* (क्षोभ्या) —$10^{17}$

- *vivaha* (विवाहा) —$10^{19}$
- *kotippakoti* (कोटिपकोटी) —$10^{21}$
- *bahula* (बहुल) —$10^{23}$
- *nagabala* (नागाबाला) —$10^{25}$
- *nahuta* (नाहूटा) —$10^{28}$
- *titlambha* (तीतलम्भा) —$10^{29}$
- *vyavasthanapajnapati* (व्यस्थानापज्नापति) —$10^{31}$
- *hetuhila* (हेतुहीला) —$10^{33}$
- *ninnahuta* (निनाहुत्ता) —$10^{35}$
- *hetvindriya* (हेत्विन्द्रिय) —$10^{37}$
- *samaptalambha* (समाप्तलम्भ) —$10^{39}$
- *gananagati* (गनानागती) —$10^{41}$
- *akkhobini* (अक्खोबिनी) —$10^{42}$
- *niravadya* (निरावाद्य) —$10^{43}$
- *mudrabala* (मुद्राबाला) —$10^{45}$
- *sarvabala* (सर्वबाला) —$10^{47}$
- *bindu* (बिन्दु or बिन्दु) —$10^{49}$
- *sarvajna* (सर्वज्ञ) —$10^{51}$
- *vibhutangama* (विभुतन्गमा) —$10^{53}$
- *abbuda* (अब्बुद) —$10^{56}$
- *nirabbuda* (निर्बुद्ध) —$10^{63}$
- *ahaha* (अहाहा) —$10^{70}$
- *ababa* (अबाबा). —$10^{77}$
- *atata* (अटाटा) —$10^{84}$
- *soganghika* (सोगान्घीक) —$10^{91}$
- *uppala* (उप्पल) —$10^{98}$
- *kumuda* (कुमुद) —$10^{105}$
- *pundarika* (पुन्डरीक) —$10^{112}$
- *paduma* (पद्म) —$10^{119}$
- *kathana* (कथन) —$10^{126}$
- *mahakathana* (महाकथन) —$10^{133}$
- *asankhyeya* (असंख्येय) —$10^{140}$

- *dhvajagranishamani* (ध्वजाग्रनिशमनी) —$10^{421}$
- *bodhisattva* (बोधिसत्व or बोधिसत्त) —$10^{37218383881977644441306597687849648128}$
- *lalitavistarautra* (ललिलातुलनातारासूत्र) —$10^{200}$infinities
- *matsya* (मत्स्य) —$10^{600}$infinities
- *kurma* (कूर्म) —$10^{2000}$infinities
- *varaha* (वराह) —$10^{3600}$infinities
- *narasimha* (नरसिम्हा) —$10^{4800}$infinities
- *vamana* (वामन) —$10^{5800}$infinities
- *parashurama* (परशुराम) —$10^{6000}$infinities
- *rama* (राम) —$10^{6800}$infinities
- *khrishnaraja* (कृष्णराज) —$10$infinities
- *kalki* (कल्कि) —$10^{8000}$infinities
- *balarama* (बलराम) —$10^{9800}$infinities
- *dasavatara* (दशावतार) —$10^{10000}$infinities
- *bhagavatapurana* (भागवतपुराण) —$10^{18000}$infinities
- *avatamsakasutra* (अवतांशकासूत्र) —$10^{30000}$infinities
- *mahadeva* (महादेव) —$10^{50000}$infinities
- *prajapati* (प्रजापति) —$10^{60000}$infinities
- *jyotiba* (ज्योतिबा) —$10^{80000}$infinities

On 7 August 2013, Vasudevan Mukunth in an article in *The Hindu* wrote about the large numbers:

> The *Jyotiba* may not make much sense today, but it represents the early days of a centuries-old tradition that felt such numbers had to exist, a tradition that acknowledged and included the upper-limits of human comprehension while on its quest to deciphering the true nature of "god".
>
> One translation, from Sanskrit to the Chinese by Shikshananda, says one *asamkhyeya* is equal to 10 to the power of 7.1-times 10-to-the-power-of-31. Another translation, to English by Thomas Cleary, says it is 10 to

the power of 2.03-times 10-to-the-power-of-32. The third, by Buddhabhadra to the Chinese again, says it is 10 to the power of 5.07-times 10-to-the-power-of-31.

## Numbers and Jainism

Jainism has contributed immensely to mathematics. The Ganitasarsangrah of Mahavira talks about 24 numbers based on the decimal system. As we all know that there were 24 prophets in Jainism, so Mahavira had specifically mentioned 24 numbers in his book. The name of numbers are—Eka (1), Das (10), Sata $(10^2)$, Sashara $(10^3)$, Das Sahasra $(10^4)$, Laksha $(10^5)$, Daslaksha $(10^6)$, Koti $(10^7)$, Das Koti $(10^8)$, Sata Koti $(10^9)$, Arbud $(10^{10})$, Nyarbuda $(10^{11})$, Kharba $(10^{12})$, Mahakharba $(10^{13})$, Padam$(10^{14})$, Mahapadam $(10^{15})$, Kshoni $(10^{16})$, Maha kshoni $(10^{17})$, Sankha $(10^{18})$, Maha Sankha $(10^{19})$, Kshiti $(10^{20})$, Maha Kshiti $(10^{21})$, Kshobh $(10^{22})$, Mahakshobh $(10^{23})$.

There is great fascination in Jain philosophy with the enumeration of large numbers, selected examples of 'time periods' mentioned include $756 \times 1011 \times 8400000028$ days, called shirsa prahelika, and 2588 years. All numbers were classified into three sets:

(a) Enumerable

(b) Innumerable

(c) Infinite

Five different types of infinity are recognized in Jaina works: Infinite in one and two directions, infinite in area, infinite everywhere and infinite perpetually.

The definitions of numerable, innumerable and infinite in Tattvārtha Sutra are obtained through a recursive process—via the distribution of mustard seeds inside the concentric rings of islands and oceans. Acharya Umāsvāt observed in *Tattvārtha Sutra: The Lower and Middle Regions*:

> There are islands and oceans that bear propitious names such as Jambu Island, Lavana Ocean, and so on. The islands and oceans are concentric rings, the succeeding ring being double the preceding one in breadth. At the centre of these islands and oceans is the round island Jambu with a diameter of 100,000 yojanas and Mount Meru at its navel.

There are seven continents on Jambu Island: Bharata, Haimavata, Hari, Videha, Ramyaka, Hairanyavata and Airavata. The six mountains that extend from east to west and divide the seven continents are Himavan, Mahahimavan, Nisadha, Nila, Rumkin and Sidharin. The mountains are, respectively, as golden as Chinese silk, as white as the Arjuna tree, as crimson as the rising sun, as blue as sapphire, as white as silver, as golden as Chinese silk.

## Number Writing System of Aryabhata

Aryabhata gave a unique method of representing huge numbers by using alphabets. He wanted to develop a system that can help him to write numbers in shloka meter. Using this method you can write big numbers with ease. Here the swara (स्वर) and vyanjana (व्यंजन) of Devnagri alphabets have been assigned different values:

क-वर्ग (Ka-Varga)

| क | ख | ग | घ | ङ |
|---|---|---|---|---|
| 1 | 2 | 3 | 4 | 5 |

च-वर्ग (Ca-Varga)

| च | छ | ज | झ | ञ |
|---|---|---|---|---|
| 6 | 7 | 8 | 9 | 10 |

## ट-वर्ग (Ta-Varga)

| ट | ठ | ड | ढ | ण |
|---|---|---|---|---|
| 11 | 12 | 13 | 14 | 15 |

## त-वर्ग (Ta-Varga)

| त | थ | द | ध | न |
|---|---|---|---|---|
| 16 | 17 | 18 | 19 | 20 |

## प-वर्ग (Pa-Varga)

| प | फ | ब | भ | म |
|---|---|---|---|---|
| 21 | 22 | 23 | 24 | 25 |

## Avarga Vyanjana (अवर्ग व्यंजन)

| य | र | ल | व | श | ष | स | ह |
|---|---|---|---|---|---|---|---|
| 30 | 40 | 50 | 60 | 70 | 80 | 90 | 100 |

## Swara (स्वर)

| अ | इ | उ | ऋ | लृ | ए | ऐ | ओ | औ |
|---|---|---|---|---|---|---|---|---|
| $10^0$ | $10^2$ | $10^4$ | $10^6$ | $10^8$ | $10^{10}$ | $10^{12}$ | $10^{14}$ | $10^{16}$ |

Aryabhata laid the whole definition in one shloka:

वर्गाक्षराणि वर्गे अवर्गे अवर्गाक्षराणि कात् ङमौ यः।
खद्विनवके स्वरा नव वर्गे अवर्गे नवान्त्यवर्गे वा।।

(Beginning with the letter Ka [क], Varga letters are to be used in Varga Place and Avarga letters are to be used at the Avarga place. Ya [य] is the sum of na [न] and ma [म] The nine vowels are to be used in two nines of places varga and avarga.)

1. According to this system, the first two notational places, the unit place and tenth place are denoted by the vowel **a**, the next two places viz. the hundred's place and the thousand's place, are denoted by the vowel **i**, the next

two places by **u**, the next two places are denoted by the vowel **r** and the next five successive pairs of places are similarly associated with the vowels **er, e, o, ai** and **au** respectively.

2. The first, third, fifth and other odd places are called varga places and the second, fourth, sixth and other even places are called avarga places.

3. It may be noted that corresponding to each vowel, there is one varga place and one avarga place. Avarga letter (consonant) ending in a particular vowel denotes the number represented by the letter occupying the varga place associated with that vowel.

4. An avarga place (consonant) ending in particular vowel denotes the number represented by the letter occupying the average place associated with that vowel.

Example:

कु = क् + उ = 1 × 10000 = 10000

ङि = ङ् + इ = 5 × 100 = 500

ङिशिबुण्लृख्यृ =

ङि = ङ् + इ = 5 × 100 = 500

शि = श् + इ = 70 × 100 = 7000

बु = ब् + उ = 23 × 10000 = 230000

ण्लृ = ण् + लृ = 15 × 100000000 = 1500000000

ख्यृ = (ख् +ष्)ऋ = (2+80) × 1000000 = 82000000

ङिशिबुण्लृख्यृ = 1582237500

## Value of Pi by Aryabhata

The ratio of the circumference of a circle to its diameter is a constant, denoted by pi. Aryabhata was the first mathematician who gave the value of pi up to four decimal places.

चतुरधिकं शतमष्टगुणं द्वाषष्टिस्तथा सहस्राणाम् ।
अयुतद्वयविष्कम्भस्यासन्नो वृतपरिणाहः ।।

Add 4 to 100, multiply by 8 and add to 62000; this is approximately the circumference of a circle whose diameter is 20000.

In simple words, a circle whose diameter is 20000 units has its circumference approximately 62832 so

π = 62832 / 20000 = 3.1416

## Value of Pi by Bhaskaracharya

व्यासे भनन्दाग्नि हते विभक्ते
खवाणसूर्यैः परिधिस्तु सूक्ष्मः ।
द्वाविंशति ध्ने विह्हतेऽष्ट शैलै :
स्थलोऽथवा सयाद्वयवहीयोग्य ।।

(For a given circle, the product of the diameter and 3927/1250 gives a good approximate value of the circumference, while the product of the diameter and 22/7 gives a rough approximation of the circumference.

In simple mathematical term

Circumference = 3927/1250 × diameter = 22/7 × diameter.)

According to this shloka in *Lilavati*, the value of pi is between 22/7 and 3927/1250.

Brahmagupta, the Indian mathematician and astronomer, took the value of pi equal to √10 whereas Mahavira has taken the value of pi to be 3.0375.

## Value of Pi in Vedic Literature

The founder of Vedic Mathematics, Swami Bharti Krishna Tirtha ji Maharaj, has given an interesting shloka which shows the value of pi up to 32 decimal places.

गोपी भाग्य मधुव्रात शृङ्गिशो दधिसन्धिग।
खलजीवित खाताव गलहालारसन्धर।।

(O Lord anointed with the yogurt of the milkmaids' worship [Krishna], O savior of the fallen, O master of Shiva, please protect me.)

The Sanskrit consonants:

ka, ta, pa, and ya all denote 1;

kha, tha, pha, and ra all represent 2;

ga, da, ba, and la all stand for 3;

Gha, dha, bha, and va all represent 4;

gna, na, ma, and sa all represent 5;

ca, ta, and sa all stand for 6;

cha, tha, and sa all denote 7;

ja, da, and ha all represent 8;

jha and dha stand for 9; and

ka means zero.

Vowels make no difference and it is left to the author to select a particular consonant or vowel at each step.

Now let's try to relate this shloka to the given system.

go/ga =3, pi/pa =1, bhag =4, ya =1, ma =5, dha =9, ra =2, ta =6 and so on.)

π = 3.14159265358979323846264338332792

The great mathematician-astronomer of Sangamagrama, Kerala, Madhava, has also tried to find the value of pi.

विबुधा नेत्रगजाहिहुताशनत्रिगुणवेदभवरणावाहवः
नवनिखर्वमिते वृतिविस्तरे परिधिमंमिदं जगदुर्बुधाः

The various words indicate certain numbers encoded in a scheme known as the bhūtasaṃkhyā system. The meaning of the words and the numbers encoded by them (beginning with the units place) are detailed in the following translation of the verse: 'Gods (vibudha : 33), eyes (netra : 2), elephants (gaja : 8), snakes (ahi : 8), fires (hutāśana : 3), three (tri : 3), qualities (guṇa : 3), vedas (veda: 4), nakṣatras (bha : 27), elephants (vāraṇa : 8), and arms (bāhavaḥ 2) — the wise say that this is the measure of the circumference when the diameter of a circle is nava-nikharva (900,000,000,000).'

According to Bhutasamkhya system a circle whose circumference is 2827433388233 will have its diameter as 900,000,000,000 gives the value of pi. This calculation yields the value $\pi = 3.1415926535922$. This is the value of pi used by Madhava in his further calculations and is accurate to 11 decimal places.

Count Magnus Fredrik Ferdinand Bjornstjerna, author of *Theogony of the Hindus,* says:

> We find in Ayeen-Akbari, a journal of the Emperor Akbar, that the Hindus of former times assumed the diameter of a circle to be to its periphery as 1,250 to 3,927. The ratio of 1,250 to 3,927 is a very close approximation to the quandrature of a circle, and differs very little form that given by Metius of 113 to 355. In order to obtain the result thus found by the Brahmans, even in the most elementary and simplest way, it is necessary to inscribe in a circle a poligon of 768 sides, an operation, which cannot be performed arithmetically without the knowledge of some peculiar properties of this curved line, and at least an extraction of the square root of the ninth power, each to ten places of decimals. The Greeks and Arabs have not given anything so approximate.

There are many more instances where you can find the reference of numbers in religious text which I couldn't highlight here. I am leaving it up to avid readers to look for more details in religious literature and unearth the mathematical richness of texts at least 1000 years ago.

# 2

# ARITHMETIC

The main source of our knowledge about mathematics in religion is the Vedas. In the very first chapter I had mentioned that the growth of number in decimal systems, sophisticated ways to write big numbers in the powers of 10, discovery of 0, concepts of infinity, addition, subtraction, etc., are evident in the Vedas and there are hundreds of reference in the Vedas where the fundamental operation of mathematics (+, −, ×, ÷) have been discussed. Even the world has accepted the fact that the counting of big numbers could not have been possible without the introduction of 10 symbols (0, 1, 2, 3, 4, 5, 6, 7, 8, and 9).

The importance of 0 cannot be understated.

Its discovery led the rest of the world to use a decimal system of notation of writing big numbers without any confusion as the place value system came to exist thereafter. The Arabs learnt the art of writing big numbers with the help of 10 notations and passed it onto the European world and it was Fibonacci who through his book *Liber Abaci* spread the message of Indian system of writing numbers to the Western world. Fibonacci in his book writes: 'When my father, who had been appointed by his country as a public notary in the customs at Bugia acting for the Pisan merchants going there, was in charge, he summoned me to him while I was still a child and having an eye to the usefulness and future convenience, desired me to stay there and receive instructions in the school of accounting. There, when I had been introduced to the art of the Indians' nine symbols through remarkable teaching, knowledge of the art very soon pleased me above all else and I came to understand it, for whatever was studied by the art in Egypt, Syria, Greece, Sicily and Provence, in all its various forms.'

Professor Ginsburg writes, 'The Hindu notation was carried to Arabia about 770 AD by a Hindu scholar named Kanka who was invited from Ujjain to the famous Court of Baghdad by the Abbaside Khalif Al Mansur. Kanka taught Hindu astronomy and mathematics to the Arabian scholars; and with his help they translated into Arabic the Brahm Sphuta Siddhanta of Brahmagupta. The recent discovery by the French savant M.F. Nau proves that the Hindu numerals were well known and much appreciated in Syria about the middle of 7th century AD.'

In the Vedas, numbers are sometimes expressed as a sum or difference of two composite numbers showing that the people at that time could do addition and subtraction as well. The number 94 in the Rig Veda is termed as 90 + 4 and 19 is expressed as 20 − 1. Swami Dayananda's *Introduction to the Commentary on Vedas* notes that the Yajur Veda not only provides proof of mantras stating the odd number sequences and arithmetical rules to derive infinite sequence but the mantras suggest the unaccountability of numbers and the decimal numbering.

In the Rig Veda, the number 3339 is spelled as three thousand, three hundred and thirty-nine. This shows that Vedic rishis were comfortable in adding two, three or four numbers at a time.

त्रीणि शता त्रीसहस्राण्यग्निं त्रिंशश्च देवा नव चासपर्यन ।
औक्षन् घृतैरसृणन् बर्हिरस्मा .......

(3339 = 33 + 303 + 3003)

This is not all. The Vedic rishis seems to be comfortable in multiplication technique too. Let's look at this sentence—

षष्टिं सहस्रानवतिं नव

This sentence talks about number 60099, and if you expand it as mentioned in the Rig Veda then you can see the formation of number using multiplication and addition.

$60099 = 60 \times 1000 + 90 + 9$

The above explanation somehow prove that they have the knowledge of decomposing a larger number into smaller and that too in power of 10 which in modern mathematical notation is called the expansion of a number in standard form. Prof S.S.N. Murthy writes that numbers above 100 don't appear to involve multiplication and the Vedic rishis were comfortable with summation of larger numbers. Though at many instances numbers in product form is also seen in the Vedas such as $3 \times 7 \times 70$. In the Puranic legend, Indra is said to have cut down the foetus in the womb of Diti into 7 pieces and again each pieces into 7 parts which shows that the number of pieces is $7 \times 7 = 49$. At many occasions in the Rig Veda 21 is written as $3 \times 7$ which is again the decomposition of a number into the product of two numbers. Sayana interpreted 21 as the sum of four numbers.

$21 = 12 + 5 + 3 + 1$

Here 12 refers to number of months in a year; 5 seasons, 3 worlds and 1 aditya (sun).

Stephen Knapp in an article 'Basic Points about Vedic Culture' points out Brihadaranyaka Upanishad, Chapter 3, Yagyavalkya has said that in reality there are only 33 gods and goddesses. And 33 is expressed as the sum of numbers as—

33 Gods = 8 Vasus + 11 Rudras + 12 Adityas (12 months are referred as 12 Adityas) +1 Indra + 1 Prajapati

Bhaskaracharya in his famous book *Lilavati* also mentions the method of addition, subtraction, multiplication and division.

कार्यः क्रमादुत्क्रमतोऽथवाङ्कयोगयो था स्थानकमंतरं वा।

The shloka directs us to write down the given number one below the other so that the digits match the place values.

In simple words, digits of every number should be placed vertically downwards to match the unit, ten's, hundred's—place of every number.

Addition or subtraction should be done place-wise from right to left or vice-versa. He also talks about multiplication and division in his book.

अये बाले लीलावती मतिमति ब्रूहि सहितान
द्विपंचद्वात्रिंशत त्रिनवतिशताष्टादश।
शतोपेतानेतानयुत वियुतांशचादि वद मे
यदि व्यक्ते युक्तिव्यवकलनमार्गेऽसि कुशला।।

(O! You smart girl 'Lilavati', if you are skillful in addition and subtraction, tell me the result when the sum of 2, 5, 32, 193, 18, 10 and 100 is subtracted from 10000.)

In Hindu religion, nine numbers refer to the nine energies, namely the seven divisions of Prakrti from Buddhi to Earth and the two descending and ascending currents of life. Thus the nine numbers complete and include all that can exist in Prakriti. The zero took birth after the union of Purusha and Prakriti.

गुण्यांत्यमंकं गुणकेन हन्यादुत्सारितेनैवमुपान्त्यमादीन्।
गुण्यस्तवधोऽधोगुणखण्डतुल्यस्तै खण्डकैः संगुणितो युतो वा।
भक्तो गुण शुध्यतियेन तेन लभ्या च गुण्यो गुणितः फलं वा
द्विधा भवेदपविभागए वं स्थानैःपृथगवा गुणितः समेतः।
इष्टोनयुक्तेन गुणेन निध्नोऽभीष्टघ्नगुण्यान्वितवर्जितो वा।।

First multiply the digit in the unit's place of the multiplicand by the multiplier, then the digit in the ten's place and so on up to the last digits on the extreme left. As far as the division process is concerned, Bhaskaracharya gives a detailed explanation of method involved in division.

भाज्याद्धरः शुद्धयति यदगुणः स्यादन्त्यात्फलं तत्खलु भागहरे।
स्मेन केनाप्यपवर्त्य हारभाज्यौ भवेद्वा सति संभवे तु।।

Find the largest integer whose product with the divisor can be subtracted from the extreme left hand digits of the dividend. This integer is the first digit of the quotient. If the divisor and the dividend have a common factor, then the common factor can be cancelled and the division is carried out with the remaining factor.

In *Lilavati*, Bhaskaracharya has described the method of squaring, cubing, extracting square root, etc. The great Indian astronomer and mathematician Aryabhata has also mentioned in his book, *Ganitapda,* a method to extract the cube root of any number, but the method is too complex to understand. The fifth shloka of Aryabhata's book *Ganitapda* reads as follows:

अघनाद भजेद द्वितीयात त्रिगुणेन घनस्य मूलवर्गेण।
वर्ग स्त्रिपूर्व गुणितः शोध्यः प्रथमाद धनस्य घनात्।।

Let us call the unit place as Ghana, the 10-place as the **First Aghana** and the 100- place as the **Second Aghana** and so on. Let us see the following table:

| 2nd Aghana | 1st Aghana | Unit |
|:---:|:---:|:---:|
| $10^2$ | 10 | 1 |
| $10^4$ | $10^3$ | — |
| — | — | — |

The steps to find the cube root of a number on the basis of the shloka are as follows:

1. Subtract the greatest possible cube from the last Ghana place.

2. Divide the second aghana place by thrice the square of the cube root already obtained in step 1.
3. Subtract from the first aghana place the square of the quotient multiplied by thrice of the previous cube root.
4. Subtract the cube of the quotient from the Ghana place.
5. Repeat the process until all the digits are exhausted.

## Cube Root Method of Aryabhata

Example: Find the cube root of 34965783

1. First place the bar on number after successive 2 digits from right.

$$3\ \overline{4}\ 9\ 6\ \overline{5}\ 7\ 8\ \overline{3}\ 3\ \overline{4}\ 9\ 6\ \overline{5}\ 7\ 8\ \overline{3}$$

2. Subtract the nearest cube ($3^3 = 27$) from the first pair (34) and place the cube root in the root result area. Copy the next digit down.

$$
\begin{array}{r}
3\ 4\ 9\ 6\ \overline{5}\ 7\ 8\ \overline{3} \\
-2\ 7\phantom{\ 9\ 6\ 5\ 7\ 8\ 3} \\
\hline
7\ 9\phantom{\ 6\ 5\ 7\ 8\ 3}
\end{array}
$$

3. Next divisor = 79. Divide it by three times the square of the current root and evaluate the quotient.
$79 \div (3 \times 3^2) = 2$ (quotient). Multiply this quotient with three times the square of first digit of cube root, i.e. $2 \times 3 \times 3^2 = 54$ and subtract it from 79.

$$
\begin{array}{r}
3\ \overline{1}\ 9\ 6\ \overline{5}\ 7\ 8\ \overline{3} \\
-2\ 7\phantom{\ 9\ 6\ 5\ 7\ 8\ 3} \\
\hline
7\ 9\phantom{\ 6\ 5\ 7\ 8\ 3} \\
-\ 5\ 4\phantom{\ 6\ 5\ 7\ 8\ 3} \\
\hline
2\ 5\phantom{\ 6\ 5\ 7\ 8\ 3}
\end{array}
$$

4. Bring down the next digit in the number to from it 256. Subtract three times the first digit of cube root times the square of the last quotient, i.e. $3 \times 3 \times 2^2 = 36$

```
3 4̄ 9 6 5̄ 7 8 3̄
-2 7
    7 9
   -5 4
    2 5 6
    - 3 6
    2 2 0
```

5. Bring down the next digit from the dividend. New dividend = 2205. Subtract the cube of last quotient from it.

```
3 4̄ 9 6 5̄ 7 8 3̄
-2 7
    7 9
   -5 4
    2 5 6
    - 3 6
    2 2 0 5
        - 8
    2 1 9 7
```

Repeat the process and you get the exact cube root.

```
3̄ 4̂ 9̄ 6̄ 5̂ 7̄ 8̄ 3̂
-2 7
    7 9
   -5 4
    2 5 6
   -  3 6           Root Result = 3 2 7
    2 2 0 5
   -      8
    2 1 9 7 7
   -2 1 5 0 4
        4 7 3 8
       -4 7 3 8
            3 4 3
           -3 4 3
                0
```

Before Aryabhata's, there was no proper method to extract the cube root of any number. All the mathematicians after him followed his method with some modifications.

The Yajur Veda mentions the series of odd numbers 1, 3, 5... 33, the arithmetical series in multiples of 4 such as 4, 8, 12, 16—48. The Taittirya Samhita describes the mathematical series with a difference of 10 or say in the multiples of 10 such as 10, 20, 30...100, or 100, 200, 300...1000 etc.

The Rig Veda discusses the number in power of 10 up to 12 and which in modern mathematical notation is nothing but the concept of indices.

In Shatapatha Brahmana, there are several instances of multiplication such as $360 \times 2 = 720$ and $720 \times 80 = 57600$.

The same book talks about the division of 720 by all integers from 2 to 23 which don't give any remainder such as—720/2, 720/3, 720/4, 720/5, 720/6, 720/8, 720/9, 720/10, 720/12, 720/15, 720/16, 720/18, 720/20 and 720/24.

The renowned professor R.L. Kashyap in a research paper *Mathematics in India of the Vedic Age* talks about the use of fractions in Vedic period. He writes that the Rig Veda (10.90) mentions the fractions ¼, ½, ¾ and also the fact that ¼ + ¾ = 1. Shatapatha Brahmana mentions the same and similar result. Mixed fractions like 1½, 2 ½, 3½ has also been mentioned in the Yajur Veda.

In *Narad Purana* there are several shlokas that explains mentions in detail the method of squaring, cubing of a number and extracting their square root and cube root. This is not all the method of solving question that involves the sum or difference of two numbers together with the product of number.

योगोऽन्तरेणोंयुर्तोअधितो राशी तु संक्रमे।
राश्यंतरहतं वर्गान्तरम योगस्ततश्च तौ।।

If the sum or difference of two numbers is known, write the sum at two places and add the difference and divide the result by 2 to get one number and subtract the difference from the sum and divide it by 2 to get the second number.

**Example 1:** If sum of two numbers is 101 and their difference is 25, what are the numbers?

**Solution:**

Write sum at two places.

101        101

Add the difference at one place and subtract the difference at another place.

101 + 25 = 126 and 101 − 25 = 76

Now, in order to get the two numbers, divide the last result by 2.

126 / 2 = 63 = first number

76 / 2 = 38 = second number

If the difference of square of two numbers as well as the difference of two numbers is known you can find the number by dividing the difference of square of number by the difference of number and get the sum of two numbers and solve as directed earlier.

**Example 2:** If the difference of two numbers is 8 and the difference of square of these numbers be 400 then find the number.

**Solution:** Difference of square / Difference of number = Sum of numbers

Sum = 400 / 8 = 50

1st Number = (50 + 8 ) / 2 = 29

2nd Number = (50 − 8) / 2 = 21

*The Narad Purana* also describes the method of finding square and square root of a number.

समांकघातो वर्गः स्यात् तमेवाहुः कृति बुधाः।
अन्त्याक्तु विषमाक्तयकत्वा कृति मूल न्स्येत्पृथक ।।

Multiplying two same numbers is called square and learned people call it kriti.

4 × 4 = 16 is the square of 4

समंत्र्यंकहतिः प्रोक्तो घनस्तत्र विधिः पदे

Multiplying same number thrice is called cubing a number.

4 × 4 × 4 = 64 is the cube of 4

Bhaskaracharya in *Lilavati* gives the method of finding squares. He writes:

समद्विघातः कृतिरुच्चेथ स्थाप्योन्त्यवर्गौ द्विगुणानत्यनिघ्नाः ।
तथाऽपरेऽङ्कास्तयकत्वान्तयमुत्सार्य पुनश्च रशिमी ।।

The product of a number by itself is a square. To square a number—first write the square of the first number and write it at the top. Multiply the next digit by the double of the first digit and write the result on the top. Next, multiply the third digit by the double of the first digit and write the result at the top. Repeat the process until you come to the unit place. Next cross the first digit and shift the number so formed one place to the right. Finally add all the products written at the top and this is the square of a number.

Algebraically,

$(a + b + c)^2 = a^2 + b^2 + c^2 + 2ab + 2bc + 2ac$

The addition and subtraction of fractions have also been discussed in *Narad Purana*.

अन्योन्यहारनियतौ हरांशो तू समिच्छदा
लवा ल्वघनाश्च हरा हरघ्ना ही सवर्णनम।
भागप्रभागे विज्ञेय मुने शास्त्रार्थचिंतकेः
अनुबन्धेऽपवाहे चैकस्य चेदधिकोनकः
भागास्त्लस्थहारेण हारं स्वन्साधिकेन तान
ऊनेन चापि गुन्येद्धनर्ण चिन्तयेत तथा

कार्यस्तुल्यहरांशानां योगश्चाप्यान्त्रो मुने ।।
अहारराशौ रूपं तू कल्प्येद्धरमप्स्थ
अंशाहतिश्छेदघातहिद्धभिन्नगुणने फलम ।।
छेदं चापि लवम विद्ल परिवर्त्य हरस्य च
शेषः कार्यों भागहारे कर्तव्यों गुणनाविधि ।।

The above method says to equate the denominator before adding or subtracting the fraction.

This shows the richness of Vedic culture which was far superior to the cultures of Greeks or Egyptians. Whatever may be the date of the Vedic hymns, whether 1500 or 15000 BC, they have their own unique place and stand by themselves in the literature of the world. They tell us something about the early growth of the human mind of which we find no trace anywhere else. The famous mathematician and historian De Morgan said, 'Hindu arithmetic is greatly superior to any which the Greeks had. Indian arithmetic is that what we use now.'

The Indian mathematician Brahmagupta, born in Ujjain in 598 AD in his book *Brahmasphutasiddhanta*, tells about the following operation:

1. The sum of zero and a negative number is negative, the sum of a positive number and zero is positive; the sum of zero and zero is a zero.
2. A negative minus zero is a negative. A positive minus zero is a positive. Zero minus zero is a zero. A negative subtracted from zero is a positive. A positive subtracted from zero is a negative.
3. The product of zero multiplied by a negative or positive is zero. The product of zero multiplied by zero is zero.
4. Zero divided by zero is zero.

In modern mathematical notation, the above laws can be written as:

i) $0 + (-a) = -a, a + 0 = a, 0 + 0 = 0$
ii) $(-a) - 0 = -a, a - 0 = a, 0-0 = 0, 0 - (-a) = a, 0 - (a) = -a$
iii) $0 \times (\pm a) = 0, 0 \times 0 = 0$
iv) $0/0 = 0$

Though the fourth law is wrong, but it was indeed a brilliant attempt on part of Brahmagupta to give the rule of mathematical operation of zero to the world.

In the Sanskrit text written below Mahivira, an Indian mathematician born around 800AD, writes about the operation of zero in his *Ganita Sara Sangraha*.

तड़ितः खेन राशिः खं सोऽविकारी हृतो युतः।
हीनोऽपि खवधादिः खंयोगे खंयोज्य रूपकम्॥

When any number is multiplied by any zero the result is zero and when any number is divided by zero the result is zero or when zero is added to or zero is subtracted from any number the result is always the same.

$a + 0 = a$      $a - 0 = a$      $a \times 0 = 0$      $a \div 0 = 0$

He is wrong here in saying that a/0 =0.

In his book *Trisatika*, Sridhar writes, 'When zero is added to any number or zero is subtracted from any number the result does not change but when any number is multiplied with zero the result is always zero.'

$a \times 0 = 0, a + 0 = a, a - 0 = a$

Sridhar didn't speak anything about a number having denominator zero. Bhaskaracharya in *Lilavati* had explicitly described the eight rules concerning zero.

योगे खं क्षेपसमं वर्गादौ खं खभाजितो राषि
खहर स्यात्खगुणः खं खगुणश्चिन्त्यश्च शेषविधौ।

If zero is added to a number, the result is the same number; the square (square, square root, cube, cube root) of zero is zero; any non-zero number divided by zero is khahara.

शून्ये गुणके जाते खं हारश्चेत पुनस्तदा राशि: ।
अविकृत व ज्ञेयस्तथैव खेनोनितश्चयुत: ।।

If a number is multiplied by zero or divided by zero the result is zero itself.

Bhaskaracharya further emphasis that any number divided by zero, it remains immutable.

It is clear from the above explanation that the information we have got from our Vedas, Puranas or any religious text was further refined by the later mathematicians and different operations in a better and planned way.

In a book *The Mystery of Mahabharata*, N.V. Thandani points out the importance of numbers 1 to 9 including 0 to be placed at the right. In Hindu religion Nine numbers refer to the nine energies, namely the seven divisions of Prakrti from Buddhi to Earth and the two descending and ascending currents of life. Thus, the nine numbers complete and include all that can exist in Prakriti. The 0 took birth after the union of Purusha and Prakriti.

## Bakhshali Manuscript

The Bakhshali manuscript is a mathematical treatise written on 70-odd leaves of birch-bark in Sanskrit in around 200–300 AD. It was discovered in 1881 in the Bakhshali village near Lahore by the tenant of an Inspector of Police named Mian An Wan Udin.

G.G. Joseph writes in *The Crest of the Peacock* (1991): 'The Bakhshali Manuscript is a handbook of rules and illustrative examples together with their solutions. It is devoted mainly to arithmetic and algebra, with just a few problems on geometry and mensuration.' Profs J. J. O' Connor and E. F. Robertson in an article on Bakhshali Manuscript say that the notation used in this book is somehow different. Fractions are not dissimilar in notation to that used today, written with one number below the other. However, no line appears between the numbers as we would write today. Another unusual feature is the sign + placed after a number to indicate a negative. It is very strange for us today to see our addition symbol being used for subtraction. As an example, here is how ¾–½ would be written.

$$\begin{array}{cc} 3 & 1+ \\ 4 & 2 \end{array} \quad \text{means 3/4 minus 1/2}$$

Compound fractions were written in three lines. Hence 1 plus ⅓ would be written as:

$$\begin{array}{c} 1 \\ 1 \\ 3 \end{array} \quad \begin{array}{l} \text{means 1 plus 1/3} \\ \text{so equals 4/3} \end{array}$$

Sums of fractions such as $^5/_1$ plus $^2/_1$ are written using the symbol yu (for yuta):

$$\begin{array}{cc} 5 & 2 \\ 1 & 1 \end{array} \text{yu} \quad \text{pha 7}$$

This means 5/1 plus 2/1 equals 7

Division is denoted by bha, an abbreviation for bhaga meaning 'part'. For example:

$$\begin{array}{l} 1 \\ 1 \quad \text{bha 8} \\ 3+ \end{array} \quad \text{pha 12}$$

This means 8 divided by 2/3 equals 12

## Square Root in Bakhshali Manuscript

अकृते श्लिष्ट कृत्यूना शेषच्छेदो द्विसंगुणः।
तदवर्ग दल संश्लिष्टः हृति शुद्धि कृति क्षयः।।

In the case of a non-square number, subtract the nearest square number, divide the remainder by twice this nearest square; half the square of this is divided by the sum of the approximate root and the fraction. This is subtracted and will give the corrected root.

$$\sqrt{Q} = \sqrt{(A^2 + b)} = A + b/2A - (b/2A)^2/(2(A + b/2A))$$

**Example:** Find the square root of 41?

**Solution:** $\sqrt{41} = \sqrt{36 + 5}$; Here A = 6 and b = 5

Hence,

$$(41)^{1/2} = 6 + \frac{5}{2 \times 6} - \frac{25}{144 \over 2\left(6 + \frac{5}{12}\right)}$$

$$= 6 + 0.41 - 0.013$$
$$= 6.397$$

*Bakhshali Manuscript*
*(Source: The Bakhshali Manuscript: An Ancient*
*Indian Mathematical Treatise by Takao Hayashi)*

## Least Common Multiple (LCM)

There is no direct reference to the LCM in Bakhshali Manuscript but the plan of reducing fractions to the least common denominator while adding or subtracting can be seen in the manuscript. In one instance, there is a problem in the book where one is required to find the sum of the fractions:

2/1, 1½, 1⅓, 1¼, 1⅕

अर्ध त्रिभाग पादांशं पंचभाग षडंश च..........ततो प्रोझ्यः सदृशं क्रियते
एषां योग कृते जात।

The simple rule to equalize the denominator is first done so as to become:

$$\frac{2}{1} + \frac{3}{2} + \frac{4}{3} + \frac{5}{4} + \frac{6}{5} = ?$$

According to Bakshali Manuscript, first we equalize the denominator and write it as:

2/1 = 120/60
3/2 = 90/60
4/3 = 80/60
5/4 = 75/60
6/5 = 72/60

Hence, sum $= \dfrac{120 + 90 + 80 + 75 + 72}{60} = \dfrac{437}{60}$

According to *The Bakhshali Manuscript: An Ancient Treatise of Indian Arithmetic* written by Swami Satya Prakash Saraswati and Dr Usha Jyotishmati, the method of finding the LCM is also been addressed in *Ganita Sara Samgraha* of Mahavira and probably also in Prithudakaswami's commentary on the Brahma-Sphuta Siddhanta but it has not been mentioned in the works of Aryabhata, Brahmagupta and Bhaskaracharya.

## Arithmetic Progression

In the Bakhshali Manuscript, there is a phrase 'rupona karanena' (रूपोना करनेण) which was used to find the sum of n terms of an arithmetical progression. The term rupona (रूप + ऊन) means one less. The word literally means deducing one. The exact use of rupona method is not available in Bakhshali but its use in Mahavira's *Ganita Sara Sangraha* is mentioned with the following verse:

रूपेनोनो गच्छो दलीकृतः प्रचयतादि तो मिश्रः।
प्रभवेन पदाभ्यस्तस्संकलितं भवति सर्वेषाम्।।

The number of terms is diminished by one, halved and multiplied by the increment. This when combined with the first term of the series and multiplied by the number of terms becomes the sum of all.

$$S = [(t-1)\ d/2 + a]t$$

## Weight and Measures

The Sanskrit terminology used in Bakhshali Manuscript to represent weight and measures is a true picture of how Indians were using weight to represent certain things. The word *chhedam* used to indicate the operation of division has been severely used in different contexts.

Chhe° 80 rakti—su° i.e. 80 raktika = 1 suvarna

Chhe° 24 am°—ha° i.e. 24 angula = 1 hasta

Chhe° 2 gha°—mu° i.e. 2 ghatika = 1 muhurta

Chhe° 4608000 ya°—yo° i.e. 4608000 yava = 1 yojana

Tolenasti dhane 12, i.e. 1 tola = 12 dhana

The Bakhshali abbreviations for weights and measures are as follows:

Adh, आ = Adhaka, आढ़क  Gav गव = Gavyuti, गव्यूति
Am, अं = Amsha, अंश  Gha, घ = Ghatika घटिका
Bha, भा = Bhara भार  Ha ह = Hasta हस्त
Di दि = Dina दिन  Kha ख = Khari खारि
Li लि = Lipta लिप्ता  Mu मू = Mudrika/ Muhurta मुद्रिका
  / मुहर्त
Pa प = Pala / Pada पल / पाद  To तो = Tola तोला

## Time Measurement

1 Varsh = 12 Moasa = 360 dina
1 Dina = 30 Muhurta = 60 Ghatika

## Arc Measures

1 Rashi = 30 Ansha = 1800 Lipta
1 Ansha = 60 Lipta
1 Lipta = 60 Vilipta

## Money Measures

1 Suvana = 1⅓ Dinara = 2⅔ Dramkshana = 16 Dhanaka = 80 Raktika
1 Dinara = 2 Dramkshana
1 Dramkshana = 6 Dhanaka
1 Dhanaka = 5 Raktika

## Weight Measures

1 Bhara = 2000 Pala
1 Pala = 8 Tola
1 Tola = 2 Dramkshan
1 Dramkshana = 6 Dhanaka
1 Dhanaka = 4 Andika

1 Andika = 1¼ Raktika
1 Raktika = 3$\frac{1}{5}$ Yava
1 Yava = 2½ Siddharatha
1 Siddharata = 2½ Kala
1 Kala = 4 Pada
1 Pada = 4 Mudrika

## Length Measure

1 Yojana = 2 Gavyuti
1 Gavyuti = 8 Krosha
1 Krosha = 1000 Dhansusha
1 Dhanusha = 4 Hasta
1 Hasta = 24 Angula
1 Angula = 6 Yava

## Capacity Measures

I Khari = 16 Drona
I Drona = 4 Adhaka
I Adhaka = 4 Prastha
I Prastha = 4 Kudava
1 Kudava = 2 Prasriti
I Prasriti =2 Pala

The Bakhshali Manuscript talks about different problems of arithmetic in detail. Some are as follows:

## Time and Distance

One goes 1½ yojana in a day and another 6 in 3 days. If the first had a start of 9 yojanas, when would the second overtake him?

## Time and Work

Two Rajputs are the servants of a king. The wages of one are two and one-sixth a day and, of the second are one and one half. The first gives to the second ten dinaras. Calculate and tell me quickly in how much time will they have equal money.

Profit and Loss

1. One buys 7 for 2 and sells 6 for 3 and 18 is his profit. What was his capital?

2. Eight articles obtained for three and six are sold for four. The sum of the capital and profit is one hundred and sixty. State o best of calculator, what was the capital and what is the profit.

**Shares and Ratio**

A certain amount given to the first, twice that to the second, thrice it to the third and four times to the fourth. State the amount given to the first and the shares of the others, if the total amount given was 200.

## Binary Operation in Pingala's *Chandasastra*

Pingala in his book *Chandasastra* has remarkably shown the height of mathematics used at that time. The text was written around 200 BC and has the reference of binary number system. Pingala describes the Gayatri metres with 6 syllables per quarter called tanumadhya. The tanumadhya (thin in the middle as the shorts are in the middle) is an even vrtta having six vranas (SS I ISS). Pingala used long (S) and short ( I) respectively for binary codes 0 and 1. In *The Prosody of Pingala* written by Dr Kapildev Dwedi and Dr Shyamlal Singh, the authors have given a detailed commentary on the way Pingala had defined binary number system. The authors point out that in order to convert the binary number system to decimal number, place 1, 2, 4, etc. beneath these varnas as follows:

|     | S   | S   | I   | I   | S   | S   |
|-----|-----|-----|-----|-----|-----|-----|
|     | 1   | 2   | 4   | 8   | 16  | 32  |

Add the numbers beneath the shorts to obtain 4 + 8 = 12. Therefore, the tanumadhya enjoys 12 + 1 = 13th place in the ordered list of 64 even vrttas. The numbers 1, 2, 4, 8, 16...are called index numbers in the context of varnic expansion, while they are called binary weights in computer system. Look at the table that gives the first 16 Pingala binary numbers along with the binary numbers in vogue. The important fact of this table is that when you reverse the order of the Pingala binary code you will get the modern binary code. Pingala has clearly mentioned अंकानां वामतो गति (the digits move in the reverse process).

| Decimal Numbers | Pingala Binary Number | | Modern Binary Numbers |
|-----------------|-----------------------|------|-----------------------|
| 0  | SSSS   | 0000 | 0000 |
| 1  | ISSS   | 1000 | 0001 |
| 2  | S ISS  | 0100 | 0010 |
| 3  | I ISS  | 1100 | 0011 |
| 4  | SS IS  | 0010 | 0100 |
| 5  | IS IS  | 1010 | 0101 |
| 6  | S I IS | 0110 | 0110 |
| 7  | I I IS | 1110 | 0111 |
| 8  | SSS I  | 0001 | 1000 |
| 9  | ISS I  | 1001 | 1001 |
| 10 | S IS I | 0101 | 1010 |
| 11 | I IS I | 1101 | 1011 |
| 12 | SS I I | 0011 | 1100 |
| 13 | IS I I | 1011 | 1101 |
| 14 | S I I I| 0111 | 1110 |
| 15 | S I I I| 1111 | 1111 |

Prof. Manjula Bhargava, an Indian-orgin Field Medal winner, in an interview to the *India Today* magazine had shown his affinity towards Sanskrit texts. He talks about the binary number discussed above as discovered by Pingala and also about the Hemchanda Number also known as Fibonacci Number. Prof Manjula says:

In the rhythms of Sanskrit poetry, there are two kinds of syllables-long and short. A long syllable lasts two beats, and a short syllable lasts one beat.

A question that naturally arose for ancient poets was: how many rhythms can one construct with exactly (say) eight beats, consisting of long and short syllables?

For instance, one can take long-long-long-long, or short-short-short-long-long-short.

The answer was discovered by the ancients, and is contained in Pingala's classical work Chandashastra, which dates back to between 500 and 200 BC.

Here is the elegant solution. We write down a sequence of numbers as follows. We first write down the numbers 1 and 2. And then each subsequent number is obtained by adding up the two previous numbers.

So, for example, we start with 1 and 2, and then 1+2 is 3, so we have so far 1 2 3. The next number is obtained by adding up the last two numbers 2 and 3, which is 5. So we have so far 1 2 3 5. The next number written is then 3+5 which is 8. In this way, we get a sequence of numbers 1 2 3 5 8 13 21 34 55 89...

The n-th number written tells you the total number of rhythms, consisting of long and short syllables, having n beats. So for 8 beats, the answer is that there are 34 such rhythms in total. This sequence of numbers is now ubiquitous in mathematics, as well as in a number of other arts and sciences! The numbers are known as the Hemachandra numbers, after the 11th century linguist who first documented and proved their method of generation—called a "recurrence relation" in modern mathematics. The numbers are also known as the Fibonacci Numbers in the West, after the famous Italian mathematician who wrote about them in the 12th century.

These numbers play an important role now in so many areas of mathematics (there is even an entire mathematical journal, the Fibonacci Quarterly, devoted to them!). They also arise in botany and biology. For example, the number of petals on a daisy tends to be one of these Hemachandra numbers, and similarly for the number of spirals on a pine cone (for mathematical reasons that are now essentially understood).

One of my favorite photographs, which I keep in my office, is of a vast field of daisies, in which every daisy has 34 petals! (Recall that 34 is the same number that appeared as the answer to our question about 8 beat rhythms, revealing a hidden connection that mathematicians now understand.)

This shows that mathematics is deep rooted in religious texts. There are several other areas mentioned in our ancient text book which could not be addressed here due to paucity of time and also the space constraints but the avid readers may find the content useful.

## Fibonacci Number

1, 1, 2, 3, 5, 8, 13, 21, 34, 55... are the Fibonacci Numbers, where every next number is the sum of the preceding two.

The instances of sun flowers with 34 and 55 florets found in the Rig Veda can be co-related with the 34 petals in one direction and 55 petals of sun flower in another direction. Here both the numbers are Fibonacci numbers. Narayana Pandita in his book *Ganita Kaumudi* (1356) studies additive sequences where each term is the sum of the last q terms. He poses the problem thus:

A cow gives birth to a calf every year. The calves become young and they begin giving birth to calves when they are three years old. Tell me, O learned man, the number of progeny produced during twenty years by one cow.

This when solved gives the Fibonacci series of number which was also dealt by Indian mathematician Gopala Hemchandra.

# 3
# ALGEBRA

Algebra seems to have been the new discovery of a mathematician but it has its origin from the Vedas. Swami Dayananda (1958) was the first to propose that algebraic idea developed from the Vedas. He cited symbols to indicate short and long vowels verses from the Sama Veda that he believed referred to the science of the unknown or variable. Swami Dayananda was of the view that the symbol used in the Vedas for unknown or variable is similar to the one used in modern mathematics. Based on the maxim that one symbol can be utilized for two purposes, Dayananda argued this as essentially an algebraic idea; a letter is used as a part of the alphabet in one sense while an unknown number or a variable in another. In Chandogya Upanishad (600 BC) the word rasi-translated is used to represent unknown amount which is equivalent to the modern use of x. It seems that *res* of Latin has been taken from the Indian word rasi having the same meaning unknown.

In ancient India, conventional mathematics termed Ganitam was known before the development of Algebra. This is the root of—Bijaganitam, which is the name of computation. Bijaganitam means the other mathematics. Bija means another or second and Ganitam means mathematics. The fact that this name was chosen for this system of computation implies that it was recognized as a parallel system of computation, different from the conventional one. The other meaning of the word Bija means seed, symbolizing origin or beginning and the inference that Bijaganitam was the original form of computation.

Stephen F Mason in his book *History of Science* published in 1962 confirmed that Vedic Indians are now credited with the development of not only our modern number system but also the development of generalized algebraic operations. On the other hand, F. Cajori in his book urges that the Indians were the first to recognize the existence of negative number.

A part of speech given by Swami Vivekanand in the Parliament of Religion in Chicago in 1893 mentioned Mathematics. Swami Vivekananda asked, 'You know how many sciences had origin in India. You are even counting 1, 2, 3, etc. to zero after Sanskrit figures and you all know that algebra also originated in India.'

The view of Dayananda made many western scholars to believe that Indian mathematics originated from the Vedas.

Fredrick Max Muller (1823–1900), a German philologist and Orientalist in his book *The Six Systems of Hindu Philosophy* published in 1899 changed his views on Hinduism after learning the research of Dayananda and he wrote:

> If I were asked under what sky the human mind has most fully developed some of its choicest gifts, has most deeply pondered over the greatest problems of life and has found solutions of some of them which well deserve the attention even of those who have studied Plato and Kant, I should point to India. And if I were to ask myself from what literature we who have been nurtured almost exclusively on the thoughts of Greeks and Romans and of the Semitic race, the Jewish, may draw the corrective which is most wanted in order to make our inner life more perfect, more comprehensive, more universal, in fact more truly human a life...again I should point to India.

Let's try to unearth the mathematical concept related to algebra which had its origin in India.

## Pascal Triangle/Meru Prastara

Blaise Pascal (1623–1662) is generally credited to have discovered the triangle-like structure used in binomial expansion but this was well discovered by Pingala. Pingala developed advanced mathematical concepts for describing prosody and in that process, he presented the first known description of binary numeral system. Pingala's work contains the base of Pascal Triangle and binomial coefficients. His works also contains the ideas of Fibonacci numbers is based on, and it seems Pingala was aware of combinatorial identity. Halayudha the tenth century commentator explains the method.

उपरिष्टादेकं चतुरस्राकोष्ठं लिखित्वा तस्याधस्तादुभतोऽर्धनिष्क्रांत कोष्ठद्वयं लिखेत्। तस्याप्यधस्तात्त्रयं तस्याधस्ताच्चतुष्टयं यावदीमितं स्थानमिति मेरूप्रस्तारः। तस्य प्रथमे कोष्ठे एक संख्या व्यवस्थाप्य लक्षणमिदं प्रवर्तयेत्। तत्र परे कोष्ठे यदेसंख्याजातं तत् पूर्वकोष्ठयोः पुर्ण निवेशयेत.............

First draw a square. Below it and starting from the middle of lower side, draw two squares on either side. Similarly draw 3, 4, 5 squares below these. Write the number 1 in the middle of the

```
                        1
                    1       1
                1       2       1
            1       3       3       1
        1       4       6       4       1
    1       5       10      10      5       1
1       6       15      20      15      6       1
    1   7   21      35      35      21  7   1
1   8   28      56      70      56      28  8   1
```

top square and inside in first and last squares of each row. Inside every other square, the number to be written is the sum of the numbers in the two squares above and overlapping it.

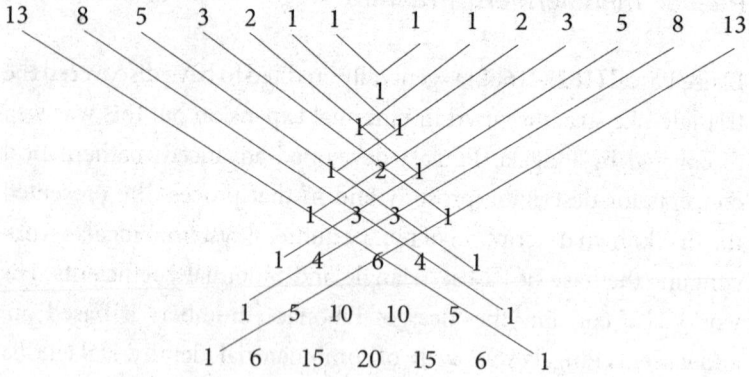

The Fibonacci numbers in Pascal's Triangle

## Unknown for Algebraic Equation

Indian algebraists were possibly the first to have used abbreviations of names or colours or gems, as symbols of unknown quantities and operations like powers, roots, etc.

| Present day notations | Ancient Times |
|---|---|
| Variables—x, y, z | Ma (Manika) <br> Ni(Indranila) <br> Mu(Mukta) |
| Operations | |
| + | Yu (Yuta) |
| − | −\| (From the Brahmi symbols for K in Ksaya |
| × | Gu (Guna) |
| / | Bha(Bhaga) |
| ( ) 2 | Va (Varga) |

| () 3 | Gha (Ghana) |
|------|-------------|
| () 4 | Va va |
| √ | Mu (Mula) |

The oldest symbols for the power of a quantity are found in the Uttararadhyaya Sutra. In it the second power is called varga (square), the third power is called ghana (cube), the fourth power is called varga-varga, and the sixth power is called ghana-varga, and the twelfth power is called ghana-varga-varga.

In the Bakhshali Manuscript, 0 is referred as the symbol for unknown quantity. B.B. Datta (1888–1958), a renowned Historian of Indian Mathematics born in Kolkata, doesn't agree with it fully but the use of the arithmetical symbol for zero in an algebraic equation is a clear proof of the want of a symbol for the unknown in the Bakhshali Manuscript. Even Sridhara and Bhaskara used the symbol looking like zero to denote the unknown.

आदि: 20 | m 0 गच्छ: 7 | गणितम् 245 |

The above is a statement of an arithmetical progression whose first term is 20, number of terms is 7, sum is 245 and whose common difference is unknown.

The lack of an efficient symbol to write an algebraic equation when more than one unknown present made it confusing.

| 0  5  यु  म  0  सा  0  7+  मू  0
| 1  1        1|       1  1       1

Which denotes $(x+5)^{1/2} = s$ and $(x-7)^{1/2} = t$

To avoid such ambiguity, in one instance in an equation with five variable, the abbreviated form of Sanskrti text of counting has been used.

प्र for prathama (प्रथम), द्वि for dvitiya (द्वितीय), तृ for tritiya (तृतीय), च for caturth (चतुर्थ) and पं for panchama (पंचम).

| 9 प्र | 7 द्वि | 10 तृं | 8 च | 11 पं | युत जातं | 16 | 17 | 18 | 19 | [20] |
| 7 द्वि | 10 तृ | 8 च | 11 पं | 9 प्र | प्रत्येक क्रमेण | | | | | |

Which means,

$$X_q + X_2 = 16, X_2 + X_3 = 17, X_3 + X_4 = 18, X_4 + X_5 = 19, X_5 + X_1 = 20$$

Bhaskaracharya in his book describes the method to know about the unknown.

उद्देशकालापवदिष्टराशिः क्षुण्णो हृतोऽशै रहितो युतो वा।
इष्टाहतं दृष्टमनेन भक्तं राशिर्भवेत्प्रोक्तमितीष्टकर्म।।

To discover the unknown number, begin with any convenient number x. Then according to conditions given in the problem, carry on the operations such as multiplication, division, etc., next multiply x by the result given in the problem and divide this product by the number obtained above. Thus we get the unknown by the method of supposition.

**Example:**

पंचघनः स्वत्रिभागोनो दशभक्तः समन्वितः।
राशित्र्यंशार्धपादेः स्यात्को राशिदर्व्युनसप्ततिः।।

A certain number is multiplied by 5 and 1/3 of the product is subtracted from he result. This is divided by 10 and to this the quotient, half, one third and one fourth of the original number are added. If this is 68, find the original number.

If we solve this question using algebra then we get x = 68.

## Progression

The Bakhshali Manuscript refers to arithmetic progression (AP). Bhaskaracharya in his book *Lilavati* has also discussed in it detail.

सैकपदध्नपदार्धमयैका़द्यकयुतिः किल संकिलताख्या।
सा द्वियुतेन पदेन विनिघ्नी स्यात् त्रिह्ता खलु संकलितैक्यम्।।

$1 + 2 + 3 + ----- + n = n (n+ 1)/2$

If you want to find the sum of n terms then multiply the last term (n) by the next term and divide it by 2.

$1 + 2 + --- + 20 = (20 \times 21)/2 = 210$

In the same manner the sum of the square of n number and sum of the "n" cube number can be extracted as described below.

द्विघ्नपदं कुयुतं त्रिविभक्तं संकलितेन हतं कृतियोगः।
संकलितस्य कृतेः सममेका़द्यंकघनैक्यमुदाह्तमाद्यैः।।

$1^2 + 2^2 + ..... + n^2 = n (n+ 1) (2n+1)/6$
$1^3 + 2^3 + ---- + n^3 = [n(n+1)]^2$

Besides, Bhaskaracharya describes the method of find the sum of n terms of an AP.

व्येकपदध्नचयो मुखयुक स्यादन्त्यधनम् मुखयुग्दलितं तम्।
मध्यधनं पदसंगुणितं तत्सर्वधनं गणितं तदुक्तम्।।

If the first term is a and the common difference is d, the nth term of the AP is given by

$$l = a + (n—1) d.$$

The sum of the n terms is given by n/2 (a + l). Here (a + l)/2 is the middle term.

This is not all, Aryabhata in his book Ganitpada writes the method to find the sum of n terms in AP.

The desired number of n terms minus one, halved, plus the number of terms which precedes, multiplied by the common difference between the terms, plus, the first term is the middle term. This multiplied by the number of terms desired is the sum of the desired number of terms.

In simple word, sum the first and last number and multiply it by the half of number of terms.

## Geometric Progression

Have you heard about the Kashi Vishwanath temple of Varanasi? It is a Sidh-pitha. The temple complex consists of a series of shrines. The linga of the main deity at the shrine is 60 cm tall and 90 cm in circumference. The main temple is a quadrangle. According to a legend, Kashi Vishwanath temple has a large room with three diamond encrusted pillars. One pillar out of three has 64 golden disks kept on one another in descending

*Kashi Vishwanath Temple, Banarasi.*
*(Source: Wikipedia)*

order. It is believed that the world will end if one moves the ring in the same order and place it in another pillar. There are two conditions associated with it:

1. Only one ring should be removed from the main pillar at a time.
2. No small ring would be placed on a large ring.

If one starts removing the ring and time taken to remove 1 ring is approximately 1 second then total time taken will be $2^{64}-1$ seconds. If one starts working 24 hours (24 × 3600 = 86400 seconds) with the help of some companions and the work doesn't stop for a year (1 year = 31536000 seconds) then it will take roughly 585 billion years to finish the work which is 127 times the current age of the sun. Here in order to calculate the timing, the formula of geometric progression (GP) is used.

This puzzle is also known as the Tower of Brahma or Tower of Hanoi. Here is a sample of Tower of Hanoi or Brahma puzzle with 8 such disks. It will take $2^8-1 = 255$ moves to shift the disk in the same order on the other pillar.

*Tower of Hanoi model with 8 discs.*
*(Source: Wikipedia)*

विषमे गच्छे व्येके गुणकः स्थाप्यः समेऽर्धिते वर्गः।
गच्छक्षयांतमंत्यात् व्यस्तं गुणवर्गजं लंय तत्।
व्येकं व्येकगुणोद्धृतमादिगुणं स्यात् गुणोत्तरे गणितम्।।

If n, the number of terms in a GP is odd then n—1 is called multiplier (M) and if it is even, n/2 is called a square(S). Now beginning with n, continue this process n-1 for odd and n/2 for even until 0 is reached. Then keep the common ratio r against 0 and start writing M or S in the opposite direction. Carry out the operations and then subtract 1 from the final result and divide it by r- 1. The result is the required sum.

Bhaskaracharya in *Lilavati* has explained about geometric progression.

**Example**: If a = 1, n = 7, r = 2, then from the above method we get the following table.

| 7 | 6 | 3 | 2 | 1 | 0 |
|---|---|---|---|---|---|
|   | M | S | M | S | M |

Beginning with 7 we write 7 – 1 = 6, we write M in 6, 6/2 = 3, 3—1 = 2, 2/2 = 1, 1—1 = 0

| 6 | M | 128 | 7 |
|---|---|-----|---|
| 3 | S | 64  | 6 |
| 2 | M | 8   | 3 |
| 1 | S | 4   | 2 |
| 0 | M | 2   | 1 |

$$S = \frac{1\ (2^7 - 1)}{2 - 1} = 128$$

## Bhaskaracharya and *Lilavati*

At the beginning of the book, Bhaskaracharya has conveyed the information on religion, the Vedas, Puranas, etc. The book begins with the praise of Lord Ganesha.

प्रीतिं भक्तजनस्य यो जनयते विघ्नं विनिघ्नन्
स्मृतस्तं वृंदारकवृंदवंदितपदं नत्वा मतंगाननम् ।
पाटी सद्गणितस्य वच्मि चतुरप्रीतिप्रदां प्रस्फुटाम्
संक्षिप्ताक्षरकोमलामलपदैलालित्यलीलावतीम् ।।

(First I offer my salutations to the elephant-faced Lord who creates love in His devotees, by remembering whom all obstacles are destroyed and whose feet are revered by the community of gods. Here I give methods of slate mathematics—*Lilavati*—which is loved by discriminating people because of its clarity, brevity as well as its literary flavour.)

In stanza 76, describes he the fighting between Arjuna and Karna during Kurukshetra War and a beautiful prose composition tells his love towards religious texts.

पार्थः कर्णवधाय मार्गणगणं क्रुद्धो रणे संदधे
तस्यार्धेन निवार्य तच्छरगणं मूलैश्चतुर्भिर्हयान् ।
शल्यं षड्भिरथेषुभिस्त्रिभिरपि च्छत्रं ध्वजं कार्मुकम्
च्छेदास्य शिरः शरेण कति ते यानर्जुनः संदधे ।।

Arjuna became furious in the war and in order to kill Karna, picked up some arrows. With half of the arrows he destroyed all of Karna's arrows. He killed all of Karna's horses with four times the square root of the arrows. He destroyed the spear with six arrows. He used one arrow each to destroy the top of the chariot, the flag and the bow of Karna. Finally he cut off Karna's bead with another arrow. How many arrows did Arjuna discharge?

Answer: If the number of arrows = $x^2$ then our equation will be:

$x^2 - x^2/2 - 4 \times = 6 + 3 + 1 = 10$

On solving, we get $x = 10$

*Lilavati of Bhaskaracharya*
*(Source: http://atributetoindia.blogspot.in/2015/05/*
*bhaskaracharyas-lilavati. html)*

This book of Bhaskaracharya has Rule of Three which is a panacea. If three quantities are known we can easily find the fourth quantity.

प्रमाणमिच्छा च समानजाति:, आद्यान्त्ययोस्ततु मध्ये तदिच्छाहतमद्ध मध्ये तदिच्छाहतमाद्यह्नतस्यात् इच्छाफलं व्यस्तवितिति।।

There are three quantities involved herein. The first one on the left (A) is called pramana (प्रमाण) or the scale, the second one (B) is called the phala (फल) or fruit and the third (C) iccha (इच्छा) or the desired result. Here A and C must be of the same kind and B should be different from A and C. Hence

$$D = \frac{B \times C}{A}$$

**Example:**

कुंकुम्स्य सदलं पलद्वयं निष्कसप्तमलवैत्रिभिर्यदि।
प्राप्यते सपदि मे वनिग्वर ब्रूहि निष्कनव्केन तत्कियत।।

**Meaning:** If two and half (Pala) of saffron cost 3/7 N(niskas), O you expert businessman, tell me quickly what quantity of saffron can be bought for 9 niskas?

**Comment:** 5 gunjas = 1 masa and 64 masas = 1 pala

so 1 pala = 320 gunjas.

The rule of three gives

$$\frac{3}{7} : \frac{5}{2} :: 9 : d$$

Hence d = 105/2 palas

The beauty of *Lilavati* is in its poetic structure where a mathematical problem has been beautifully written in 2 lines, 3 lines or 4 lines. It personifies mathematics. Let's see one problem on finding an unknown where a small quarrel between a husband and a wife has been beautifully written in poetic lines.

हारस्तारस्तरूण्या निधुवनकलहे मौक्तिकानां विशीर्णो
भूमौ यातस्त्रिभागः शयनतलगतः पंचमांशोऽस्य दृष्टः ।
प्राप्तः षष्ठः सुकेशया गणक दशमकः संगृहीतः प्रियेण
दृष्टं षटकं च सूत्रे कथय कतिपयैमौक्तिकैरेष हारः ।।

In a coital spot of a couple, the lady's pearl necklace was broken. One-third of the pearls fell on the ground, one-fifth went under the bed. The lady collected one-sixth and her lover collected one-tenth. Six pearls remained on the original thread. Find the total number of pearls in necklace?

Answer: 30

Bhaskaracharya has also discussed the topic of permutation and combination at length. Let's see a beautiful problem on Lord Shiva based on combination.

पाशांकुशाहिडमरूककपालशूलैः खट्वांगशक्तिशरचापयुतैर्भवन्ति ।
अन्योन्यहस्तकलितैः कति मूर्तिभेदाः शंभोर्हरेरिव गदारिसरोजशंखैः ।।

Lord Shiva holds ten different weapons, namely a पाश (trap), अंकुश (goad), सर्प (snake), डमरू (drum), कपाल (potsherd), त्रिशुल (club), खट्वांग (pear), शक्ति (missile), तीर (arrow) and धनुष (bow) in his hands. In how many ways can Lord Shiva's idol be made with these weapons in his hand?

Ans = 10! = 10 × 9 × 8 × ---- 2 × 1 = 3628800

*Lord Shiva with 10 weapons in 10 hands*
*(Source: Mathematics in Ancient India, NCERT)*

The absolute beauty of mathematics can't be imagined without the discovery by Indians. Since the Vedic period algebraic concepts started making its root. Mathematicians like Aryabhata, Brahmagupta, Bhaskaracharya, Mahavira, Sridhara, Kerala School of mathematicians all have done a remarkable job to make India a nation where mathematics has been worshiped as God.

# 4
# GEOMETRY

Vedic mantras are potent sources of power and energy. The oldest book of the world known as the Rig Veda consists of mantras in praise of deities like Maruts, Brahaspati, Rudra, Mitra, Varun, Soma, Yama and other gods giving prominence to Agni, Indra and Aditya.

वेदा हि यज्ञार्थमभिप्रवृत्ताः कालंनूपूर्व्या विहिताश्च यज्ञाः।
तस्मादिदं कालविधानशास्त्रयो ज्योतिषं वेद स वेद यज्ञान।।

(This science of astronomy exits only to fix suitable times and he who knows astronomy will also know yajnas.)

The Kausitaki Brahmana of the Rig Veda mentions that the Yajur Veda and Sama Veda have emanated from the Rig Veda. The Yajur Veda basically tells the procedure, rules and regulations governing sacrifice for conducting various rites to please gods. There are two divisions of the Yajur Vedas called Krishna (Black) Yajur Veda and Shukla (White) Yajur Veda. In the Krishna Yajur Veda, the Samhita and Brahmana are not separate entities whereas in the Shukla Yajur Veda there is a clear distinction between Samhita and Brahmana. The Samhita consists of shlokas and mantras in praise of various deities and the Brahmanas deal with the procedures to be adopted for doing yagnas.

The Shukla Yajur Veda originally had fifteen sakhas out of

which only two sakhas or branches, called Madyandina and Kanva Sakhas are available at present. In both sakhas, the Brahmana is called Sathapatha Brahmana. The Samhitas and Brahmanas are considered as apaurusheya (अपौरुषेय) meaning not created by man but revealed to him by God. The Brahmanas elaborate the procedures to construct altars which involve very detailed geometry and also mentions a system of remembering the number of times a sacrifice is to be made. The numbers some time run to thousand and millions and hundred millions. It shows the highly evolved system of arithmetic and geometry during the Vedic period! This arithmetic and geometry came in handy in constructing the temples of gigantic proportions without any fault.

## Geometry in Vedas

The following verse from the Rig Veda (Mandala 10, Sukta 130, Verse 3) deals with the creation of the universe.

- Who was the measurer *prama*?
- What was the model *pratima*?
- What were the building materials for things offered *nidanam ajyam*?
- What is the circumference/*paridhih* of this universe?
- What are the meters or harmonies behind the universe *Chhandah*?

In the Atharva Veda (10.2.31) the town of gods called Ayodhya (now in Uttar Pradesh)is described. It is circular in plan with eight rampart walls and nine doors. The Atharva Veda (19.58.4) also mentioned that the town was made unconquerable using the ayasa.

Chariots are mentioned copiously in the Rig Vedas. The hymns 1.118.2 and 1.34.2 of the Rig Veda say that chariots could also be triangular having three seats and three wheels. The spoked wheel is mentioned in many places in the Rig Veda—five spoked wheels (1.164.13) and the 360-spoked wheels (1.164.48). Dr R.P. Kulkarni in his book *Geometry According to Sulba Sutra* (1983) writes:

'The proficiency in chariot building presupposes a good deal of knowledge of geometry...the fixing of spokes of odd or even numbers require knowledge of dividing the area of the circle into the desired numbers of small parts of equal area, by drawing diameters. This also presupposes the knowledge of dividing a given angle into equal parts.'

This clearly shows that a sound knowledge of geometry was also known to the people during the Vedic period.

As George Frederick William Thibaut the author of *Mathematics in the Making in Ancient India*, remarked:

The want of some rule by which to fix the right time for the religious altar gave the first impulse to astronomical observations; urged by this the priest, remained watching night after night the advancement of the moon through the circle of the Nakshatras...The laws of phonetics were investigated....the wrong pronunciation of a single letter of the text; grammar and etymology had the task of securing the right understanding of the holy texts. And Thibaut then lays down the principle, which should never be overlooked by Indian historians, that whatever science "is closely connected with the Ancient Indian religion, must be considered as having sprung up among the Indians themselves, and not borrowed from other nations".

Brahmanas are available amongst the branches of the Krishna Yajur Veda and Shukla Yajur Vedas known as Sathapatha Brahmana. According to an article published on *Encyclopedia Web Portal*, in Satapatha Brahmana there is an interesting sequence of divisions of 720 bricks into groups of successively smaller quantities, with the explicit exclusion of all divisors that are multiples of numbers which are relatively prime to 60 (i.e., their only common divisor is 1).

As far as geometry during the Vedic period is concerned, the main source of knowledge is attributed to Sathapatha Brahmana and Sulbasutra. The shlokas in the Vedas were used for sacrificial rites which were conducted to please gods. There were food and animal sacrifices at the alter as well. The Sulbasutra is about appendices to the Vedas which give rules for constructing altars. For making the sacrificial rituals a success, the altar had to be of precise measurement. Now let's come to the actual meaning of Sulbas sutras.

B. B. Dutta says the following words about the Indian geometry, in his book *Hindu Geometry* co-authored by A.N. Singh:

> ...One who was well versed in that science was called in ancient India as samkhyajna (the expert of numbers), parimanajna (the expert in measuring), sama-sutra-niranchaka (uniform-rope-stretcher), Shulba-vid (the expert in Shulba) and Shulba-pariprcchaka (the inquirer into the Shulba). Of these terms, viz. 'sama-sutra-niranchaka' perhaps deserves more particular notice. For we find an almost identical term, 'harpedonaptae' (rope-stretcher) appearing in the writings of the Greek Democritos (c. 440 BC). It seems to be an instance of Hindu influence on Greek geometry. For the idea in that Greek term is neither of the Greeks nor of their acknowledged teachers in the science of geometry, the Egyptians, but it is characteristically of Hindu origin. The English word 'Geometry' has a Greek root which itself is derived from the Sanskrit word 'Jyamiti'. In Sanskrit 'Jya' means an arc or curve and 'Miti' means correct perception or measurement.

Geometry was previously known as sulba. It was also known as rajju. In Manava Sulba and Maitrayaniya Sulba, we get the name sulba vijyana, which means science of the sulba. The sanskrit word sulba or rajju means a rope or a cord.

Geometrical rules found in the Sulbasutra, therefore, refer to the construction of squares and rectangles, the relation of the diagonal to the sides, equivalent rectangles and squares, equivalent circles and squares, conversion of oblongs into squares and vice versa, and the construction of squares equal to the sum or difference of two squares. Thus, a prior knowledge of the Pythagoras Theorem is disclosed.

In Sulbasutra, the rectangular figure was also named in accordance with the number of sides of figures—tribhuja (triangular), catur bhuja (quadrilateral) and panch bhuja (pentagon). This is not the end of the story. Vedic scholars also used to name figures on the basis of angles. In the Katyayana Sulba, we find the terms trikarna (triangle) and panch karna (pentangle). Here the word karna means angle. Triangles were classified in accordance with the sides: sama-tribhuja (equailateral

*Fire sacrifice*
*(Source: Wikipedia)*

triangle), dwisama-tribhuja (isosceles triangle) and visama-tribhuja (scalane triangle). Naming the triangle on the basis of angle is not mentioned anywhere, though Brahmagupta named jatya-tribhuja for right angle. In the Taittriya Samhita (3000 BC), the Brahmana (2000 BC) and the Brahmprauga (2000 BC) and also in the Sulba, an isosceles triangle is known as prayuga derived from the word pra + yuga meaning the fore part of the shafts of a chariot. A rhombus was similarly called ubhayatah prayuga.

Sulba means pieces of chord or string and sutra means formula. The sulbasturas are the mathematical discoveries by famous Indian rishis around 1000 BC to 200 BC, who used a piece of chord for constructions of various fire sacrifice altars.

The rituals of sacrifice as mentioned in Vedic texts are as follows:

- The soma rituals involved the extraction, utility and consumption of soma.
- Fire rituals involved the agnihotra or oblation to Agni and the Agnicayana. The sophisticated rituals of pilling the fire altar.
- The ashvamedha or yajna was dedicated to the glory, well-being and prosperity of the kingdom.

So far seven different Sulbasutras have been identified by scholars. They are as follows:

1. Baudhayana Sulbasutra
2. Apastamba Sulbasutra
3. Katyayana Sulbasutra
4. Manava Sulbasutra
5. Maitrayana Sulbasutra
6. Varaha Sulbasutra
7. Vadhula Sulbasutra

Amongst the seven mentioned above, Bodhayana Sulbasutra is considered to be the most ancient one. Bodhayana Sulbasutra is made up of 3 chapters constituting about 520 sutras. The first chapter has 113, the second chapter has 83 and the third chapter has 323 sutras written in a very systematic manner. The Baudhayana Sulbasutra was written around 800 BC. In early geometry, the circle was termed as mandala (round), pari mandala (round on all the sides), the circumference as parinaha and the diameter as vyasa or viskambha. Mahidhara in on Katyayanasulbasutra described the qualities of Sulbakara in the following verse.

संख्याज्ञः परिमाणज्ञः समसूत्रनिरऋछकः ।
समसूत्रौ भवेद्विद्वान् शुल्बवित् परिपृच्छकः ।।
शास्त्रबुद्धिविभागज्ञः परशास्त्रकुतूहलः ।
शिल्पिभ्यः स्थपतिभ्यश्चाप्याददीत मतीः सदा ।।
तिर्यगान्याश्च सर्वार्थः पार्श्वमान्याश्चयोगवित ।
करणीनां विभागज्ञः नित्योद्युक्तश्च सर्वदा ।।

A sulbakara (a person well-versed in the Sulbasutra) must have sound knowledge of arithmetic and mensuration. He must be an inquirer, quite knowledgeable in his own discipline. He must be enthusiastic in learning other disciplines, always willing to learn from practicing sculptors and architects and must be industrious.

All the seven Sulbasutras basically define the rules to construct altars with precision to please gods. The people made sacrifices to their gods so that the gods might be pleased and give them plenty of foods, good fortune, good, health, material benefits and long life. In order to please the gods the altar had to be of accurate length and area. The altars were of different shapes for fulfillment of different types of wishes.

छन्दश्चितं चिन्वीत पशुकामः पशवो वै छन्दांसि पशुमानेव भवति ।
श्येनचितं चिन्वीत स्वर्गकामः श्येनो वै वयसां प्रतिष्ठा

श्येन एव भूत्वा स्वर्गं पतति।
प्रौगचितं चिन्वीत भ्रातृव्यवान् प्रैव भ्रातृव्यान् नुदते .....

| Name of the citi | Shape | Who has to perform |
|---|---|---|
| छन्दश्चितं | Form of a bird | Desirous of cattle |
| श्येनचितं | Form of a bird | Desirous of heaven |
| प्रौगचितं | Isosceles triangle | Annihilation of rivals |
| रथचक्रचिति | Chariot wheel | Desirious of region |
| द्रोणचिति | Form of a trough | Abundance in food |

Source: NPTEL Course: Vedas and Sulbasutras by K. Ramasubramanian—IIT Bombay

The Sulbasutras deal with the correct construction of the vedi and agni including orientation, size, shape and areas and, as such, they are not meant as mathematical theorems or proofs. In the early Hindu geometry, a plane surface bounded by the figure was called the ksetra and its area, bhumi. A curved surface was called prstha (back). The geometry in the Sulbasutras can be categorized into that which expressly states theorems, constructions and implicit geometrical truths contained in constructions.

The various forms of altars as mentioned in Taittiriya Samhita of the Krishna Yajur Vedas are as follows:

- Syenaciti (in the shape of a hawk)—for attaining heaven because the hawk is the best flier among the birds
- Kankaciti (in the shape of a heron)—for progress in heaven
- Alajaciti (in the shape of a alaja bird)—for reputation in heaven
- Praugaciti (in the shape of an isosceles triangle)—for repelling foes
- Ubhayatah-Praugaciti (in the shape of a Rhombus)—for repelling present and future enemies
- Rathacakraciti (in the form of a chariot wheel)—for defeating enemies

- Dronaciti (in the form of a trough- square or circular)—for gaining food
- Samuhyaciti (in the form of a circle)—for gaining herds of cattle
- Paricayyaciti (in the form of a large circle)—for gaining village
- Smasanaciti (cemetery altar in the form of a trapezium)—for success in the world of forefathers

Besides there are Dashinagni (in the shape of a semicircle) and Kurmaciti (in the shape of a tortoise)—which are constructed by one who desires victorious career in Brahmaloka (the abode of Lord Brahma).

In an article published in the *Indian Journal of History of Science* (2003) titled 'Agni Kundas—A Neglected Area of Study in the History of Ancient Indian Mathematics', R. C. Gupta cites that the people during the Vedic era used to make different geometrical-shaped altars according to their desires such as:

- Square kunda for overall success (Sarvasiddhi)
- Yoni kunda (whose shape resembles a leaf of the pipal tree) for the birth of a son.
- Semi-circle (in the form of a half-moon)—for general good and auspiciousness
- Equilateral triangle for destruction of one's foes
- Regular hexagon for subjugation and killing of enemy
- Circular kunda for peace and removal of evil effects
- Lotus-shaped for enrichment and rain
- Regular octagon for health and freedom from disease

The Taittriya Samhita states: 'He who desires heaven, may construct falcon-shaped altar, for falcon is the best flyer among the birds.' It seems that such information is superfluous but it has actually led to important contribution in geometry and mathematics. A.K. Bag, in an article an article published in the *Indian Journal of History of Science* of Science entitled 'Ritual Geometry in India and its Parallelism in other Cultural areas', writes that the construction of altars having drawn on a base of different figures such as square, circle, semi-circle, isosceles trapezium, triangle, rhombus, falcon or tortoise shape and other led to the development of various geometrical figures, their transformations and calculation of areas involving many Pythagorean relations with rational and irrational numbers leading to its general statement, approximation of the value of $\sqrt{2}$ and others. Tackling of geometrical and mathematical problems with irrational numbers was indeed a unique achievement of the early Indian mathematicians. They had not only developed the technical terms like dvikarani ($\sqrt{2}$), dvitiyakarani ($1/\sqrt{2}$), tr-karani ($\sqrt{3}$), tritya- karani ($1/\sqrt{3}$), panca- karani ($\sqrt{5}$) and pancama-karani ($1/\sqrt{5}$), etc., but actually understood the significance.

There is a lot of data available on Sulbasutra, but the work done by Satapatha Brahmana seems to have been forgotten. Professor Subhash K. Kak of the Louisiana State University describes the altar construction in the agnicayana rite. Agni is the year; therefore, this rite is about a representation of the reckonings of the year.

अग्नये इदं न मम ।
(This if for Agni, not for me)

This rite was performed for 12 days; each day representing one month. This 12-day agnicayana rites used to take place in a large trapezoidal area, called Mahavedi, and in a smaller rectangular area to the west of it, called the pracinvavamsa or pragvamsa.

'Man is unborn as long as he has not yet established the fire, he is born only when establishes the fire.

'Agni is the central feature of the Vedic world and there are more than 200 hymns of the Rig Veda addressed to Agni.

'Agni is brilliant, golden, has flaming air and beard, three or seven tongues, his face is light, his eyes shine, he has sharp teeth, he makes a cracking noise, and leaves a black trial behind. He is fond of clarified butter, but he also easts wood and devours the forest in fact he eats everything. He is in particular a destroyer of demons and a slayer of enemies.'

The season for performing Agnicayana rite is spring. As far as the Mahavedi construction is concerned, it is described as follows:

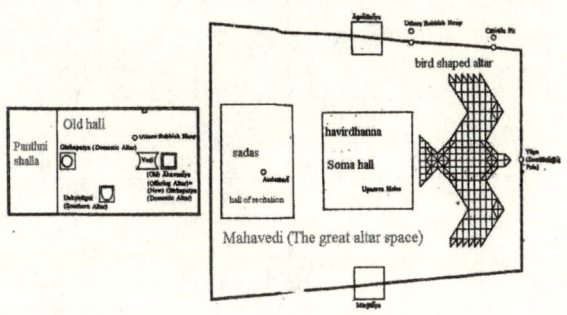

*(Source: http://www.athirathram.org/concepts.html)*

1. Sadas—Hall of recitation
2. Agnidhriya and Marjaliya Shed—In a square shape
3. Shelter house of cows
4. Abavaniya or offering altar built in the shape of a bird

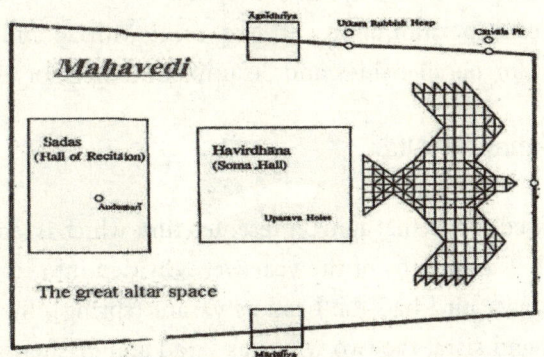

*(Source: http://www.athirathram.org)*

In the Agnicayana ritual, the Mahavedi has a length of 24 prakrama in the east, 30 in the west and 36 in the north and south.

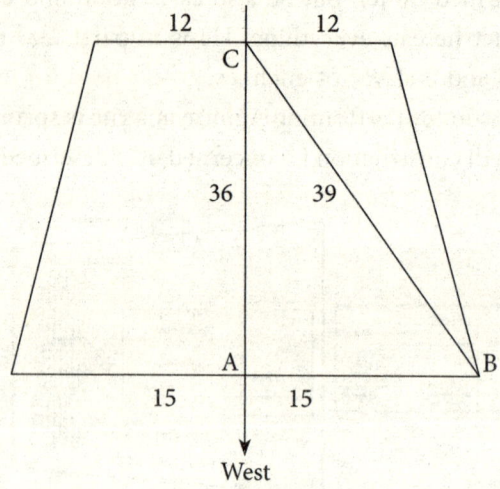

The choice of these numbers appears to have been related to the sum of these three equalling one-fourth the year or 90 days. In the Mahavedi, a brick altar is built to represent time in the form of a falcon about to take wing, and in the pracinavamsa, there are three fire altars in specified positions, the garhapatya, ahavaniya and daksinagni. Thus a mahavedi (अष्टविंशत्यूनं पदसहस्रं महावेदिः) is an isoscles trapezium of area 972 sq. units with 24 and 30 units of length for parallel sides and 36 units of length for altitude.

## Falcon-shaped Altar

As discussed above, that agni represented time which is represented by a bird. The months of the year were divided into six seasons. The year as a bird had the head as vasant (spring), the body as hemanta and sisra, the two wings as sarad and grisma (summer) and the tail as varsa (monsoon) (Taittiriya Brahamana 3.104.1).

It was believed that offering a sacrifice on such an altar would enable the soul of a supplicant to be conveyed directly to heaven by a falcon. An altar in the shape of a falcon used to be constructed in 5 layers with 200 bricks for each layer making the total number of bricks 200 × 5 = 1000 bricks. The bricks used for the platform were of 5 different shapes. These bricks were made by a special class of experts. No burnt bricks were used for the purpose. Only sun-dried bricks were used for constructing the altar.

*Five different shapes of bricks used to construct a falcon-shaped altar*
*(Source: www.athirathram.org)*

The basic structure of the bricks used to be a square which were further divided into different shapes for the purpose. The dimension of chaturthi bricks are as follows:

The basic falcon-shaped altar had an area of 7½ sq. purusha while the body of the falcon-shaped altar was 2 × 2 = 4 square purusas, the wings and the tail were one square purusha each. To make the shape look like a bird the wings were lengthened by

*Chathurthi, square-shaped*
Size: 30 angulas × 30 angulas

*Trasra padya, Triangular quarter*
Size: 30 × 15√2 × 15√2 angulas

*Chathurthhyardha, half of a square*
Size: 30 × 30 × 30 √2 angulas

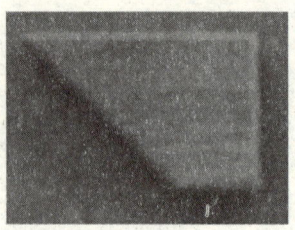

*Chathurasrapadya*
Size: 22½ × 15 × 7½ × 15√2 angulas

*Hamsamukhi*
Size: 22½ × 15 × 7½ × 15√2 angulas

*(Source: www.athirathram.org)*

one-fifth of a purusa and the tail used to be one-tenth of a purusa.

Thus, the total area of the top layer is = 4 + (2 × 1.2) + 1.1 = 7.5 square purushas or approximately 30m$^2$.

The area of the second layer got increased by one square purusha, i.e., 8½ purushas. Similarly, each successive layer was increased by 1 square purushas until the area of the base of this huge construction would be 101.5 square purushas or about 400m$^2$. It is important to note that there should be 95 altars in sequence.

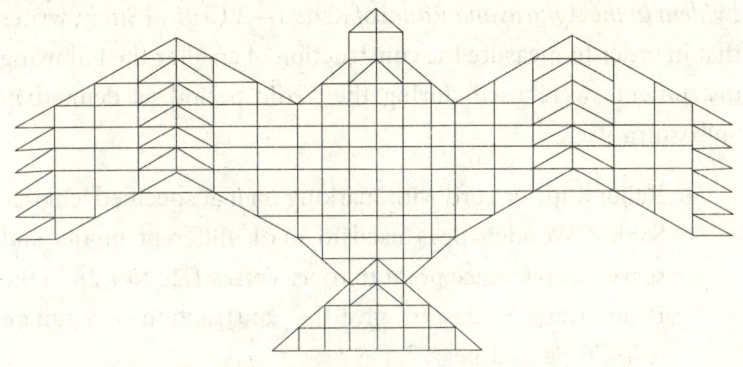

*The falcon-shaped altar called Syenaciti*
*(Source: Mac Tutor Archive)*

## Number of Bricks Used

As discussed earlier, a falcon-shaped altar requires 200 bricks in each layer and the distribution of bricks to make the shape has also been described by rishis in Satpatha Brahmins.

एवं षट्चत्वारिंशदात्मनि। शिरसि चतुर्दश। द्वात्रिंशत्पुच्छे। पक्षयोरष्टशतम्। अस्मिन् प्रस्तारे नवषष्टिचतुर्थ्यः। अर्धा द्वासप्ततिः पाद्या द्विपंचाशत्। षट् चतुरश्रपाद्या। ए का हंसमुखी।

| Parts | $B_1$ | $B_2$ | $B_3$ | $B_4$ | $B_5$ | TOTAL |
|-------|-------|-------|-------|-------|-------|-------|
| Head  | –     | 10    | –     | –     | –     | 10    |
| Body  | 12    | 28    | 4     | –     | 4     | 48    |
| Wings | 48    | 28    | 34    | –     | –     | 110   |
| Tail  | 8     | 4     | 18    | –     | 2     | 32    |
| Total | 68    | 70    | 56    | –     | 4     | 200   |

## Measuring Instruments of Sulbasutra

D.S. Sivanandan, in *The Continuity of Sulbasutra Tradition as*

*Evident in the Agnicayana Ritual of Kerala—A Critical Study,* writes that in order to measure the construction of an altar the following instruments were used during the Vedic period as defined in Sulbasutra itself.

- Rajju: Rope or cord with marking on it at specified lengths.
- Sanku: Wooden pegs used to mark different points and served as reference point to rope. Verses 1.22 to 1.28 in the Baudhayana Sulbasutra give the construction of a square using rope and pegs.
- Venu: Bamboo pole with length equivalent to the height of Yajamana, at raised hands position. This is usually taken as 1 purusha which is 120 angulam.
- Shamya: A wooden yoke-pin of length 36 angulum.

As far as measurement of altar is concerned the Sulbasutra talks about the units in the same sense as that were used earlier in the Samhitas and other Vedic literature. The units like angula, pada, prakrama, pradesa, bahu and aratni were common during that period and these terms reveal that these were coined from the body measures commonly used in daily life. It is important to note here that these units were sometimes used to represent areas. D. S. Sivanandan mentions the following measuring units of Sulbasutra.

1. Angulam = width of 14 anu = 34 tila arranged side by side, or the width of the middlemost joint of the middle finger of a man of medium size may be taken to be equal to an angulam
2. 1 ksudrapadam= 10 angulam
3. 1 pradesam = 12 angulam
4. 1 pritha= 13 angulam
5. 1 padam= 15 angulam
6. 1 eesham= 188 angulam

7. 1 aksham= 104 angulam
8. 1 yuga= 86 angulam
9. 1 janu= 32 angulam
10. 1 shamya= 36 angulam
11. 1 prakramam= 30 angulam = 2 padas
12. 1 aratini= = 2 pradesas = 24 angulam
13. 1 purushan= 5 aratnis = 120 angulam
14. 1 vyayamam= = 4 aratnis = 96 angulam

The unit pada (foot) is equal to 10 or 12 angulas.

The bricks used in altar construction were of two types—ordinary (lokamprna) and special (yajusmati). Suhash C. Kak in an article 'Astronomy of Satapatha Brahmana' published in *Indian Journal of History of Science*, 28 (1), 1993, writes that total number of yajusmati bricks described in Satapatha Brahmana was 395. This was due to 360 days of the year and 36 additional (including one being the filling between the bricks) days of the intercalary month.

The total number of lokamprna bricks is 10800, which equals the number of muhurtas in a year (1 day = 30 muhurtas). Of these 21 go into the garhapatya, 78 into the eight dhisnya hearths, and the rest go into the ahavaniya altar. The fire altars are surrounded by 360 enclosing stones; of these 21 are around the garhapatya, 78 around the dhisnya and 261 around the ahavaniya. The ahavaniya includes the dhisnya therefore the number of days assigned exclusively to the ahavaniya is 261–78 = 183 days which is equal to the days of the uttarayana of a 366 day year (now called leap year). The choice of the 21 days for the garhaptya is from the unique symbolism of 12 months + 5 seasons + 3 worlds + 1 sun.

The choice of 21 days may also refer to 5 mahabhutas (earth, water, fire, air, space) + 5 breaths (prana, apana, vyana, udana, samana) + 5 jnanedriyas (organs of cognition) + 5 karmendriyas (organs of action) + the antahkarna (the inner air).

## Important Geometrical Result Mentioned in Sulbasutra

The Sulbasutra talks about several geometrical theorems used for the construction of altars to perform yagna. Some of them are as follows:

1. The diagonal of a rectangle divides it into two equal parts.
2. The diagonals of a rectangle bisect each other and opposite areas are equal.
3. The perpendicular through the vertex of an isosceles triangle on the base of the triangle divided the triangle into two equal parts.
4. A rectangle and a parallelogram on the same base and between the parallels are equal in area.
5. The diagonals of a rhombus bisect each other at right angles.
6. The area of a square by joining the midpoints of the sides of a square is half of that of the original square.
7. A quadrilateral formed by the lines joining the midpoints of the sides of a rectangle is a rhombus whose area is half of that of the rectangle.
8. The tangents to a circle are perpendicular to the radius at the point of contact.
9. A finite line can be divided into any number of equal parts.
10. The perpendicular bisector of a line is the locus of points equidistant from the end point of the line.
11. The line joining the vertex to the middle point of the base of an isosceles triangle is perpendicular to the base.
12. The area of an isosceles triangle is equal to half the area of the rectangle with sides equal to the base and the altitude of the triangle.

Sulbasutra demonstrates the high quality of mathematical

knowledge the people of that time were having. The preciseness to determine many mathematical problems at that time shows the height of geometrical knowledge of rishis. The following are some of the important construction used in Sulbasutra:

1. To divide a line segment into any number of equal parts.
2. To divide a circle into any number of equal areas by drawing diameters (Baudhayana Sulbasutra).
3. To divide a triangle into a number of equal and similar areas (Baudhayana Sulbasutra).
4. To draw a straight line at right angles to a given line.
5. To draw a straight line at right angles to a given line from a given point on it.
6. To construct a square on a given side.
7. To construct a rectangle of given length and breadth (Baudhayana Sulbasutra).
8. To construct an isosceles trapezium of given altitude, face and base (Baudhayana Sulbasutra).
9. To construct a parallelogram having the given sides at a given inclination.
10. To construct a square equal to the sum of two different squares (Baudhayana Sulbasutra).
11. To construct a square equivalent to two given triangles.
12. To construct a square equivalent to two given pentagons.
13. To construct a square equal to a given rectangle in area (Baudhayana Sulbasutra).
14. To construct an isosceles trapezium having a given face and equivalent to a given square or rectangle.
15. To construct a rectangle having a given side and equivalent to a given square (Baudhayana Sulbasutra).
16. To construct a triangle equivalent to a given square.
17. To construct a square equivalent to a given isosceles triangle.

18. To construct a rhombus equivalent to a given square or rectangle (Baudhayana Sulbasutra).

19. To construct a square equivalent to a given rhombus.

Some of the problems discussed later will help you to understand the extent of mathematical expertise involved in construction of altars.

## Determination of East-West Line:

The oldest description of the Indian Circle Method to determine the East-West line is described in Katyayana Sulbasutra. The determination of direction was necessary to construct the Vedic fire altars.

समे शंकु निखाय शंकुसम्मितया रज्जवा मण्डलं परिलख्य यत्र लेखयो: शंक्वग्रच्छाया निपतति तत्र शंकु निहन्ति सा प्राची।

Driving the gnomon (shadow pointer) into the levelled (ground), and drawing a circle with the rope whose length is equal to the gnomon (length), one drives two pegs at (the intersections of) the two lines where the shadow of the tip of the gnomon falls. This is the east-west line.

In other words, fasten a stick (gnomon) on a water-levelled surface and draw a circle with radius identical to the height of the gnomon. In the morning and in the afternoon mark where the shadow of the sun crosses the circle: these two marks are orientated east-west.

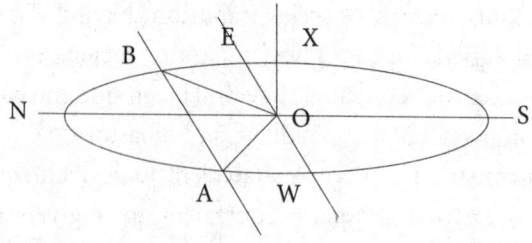

*OA = Forenoon Shadow    OB = Afternoon Shadow*

## To draw a perpendicular bisector of a given line:

Sulbasutra discussed two methods for obtaining perpendicular bisector of a line. They are:

- Folding the cord (रज्ज्वभ्यसनम्)
- Drawing fish-figure (मत्स्यचित्रणम्)

Katyayana and Manava Sulbasutra described two methods to draw a perpendicular bisector of a line.

तदन्तसं रज्वाभ्यस्य, पाशौ कृत्वा, शंक्वोः पाशौ प्रतिमुच्य,
दक्षिणायम्य मध्ये शंकु निहन्ति।
एव मुत्तरतः, सोदीची।

In modern mathematics language, it can be said in the following words: Let AB be the given line. Construct identical isosceles triangles ABC and ABD on either side of the given line AB. Join CD. Let the line CD intersect the given line AB at O. The line COD is the perpendicular bisector of the line AB.

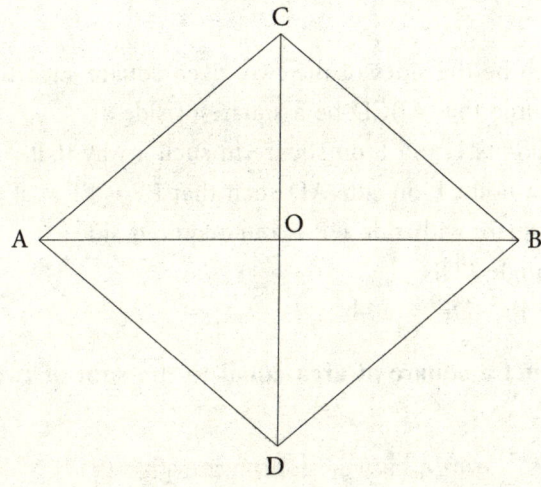

**To construct a square whose area is equal to the difference of two squares:**

In Baudhayana, there is also a reference to constructing a square whose area is equal to the difference of two squares which is evident in the following verse.

चतुरश्राच्चतुरश्रं निजिहीर्षन् यावन्निचिहीर्षेत
तस्य करण्या वृध्रमुल्लिखेत् ।
वृध्रस्य पार्श्वमानी अक्षणया इतरत्
पार्श्व उपसंहरेत् सा यत्र निपतेतदपछिन्धात् ।

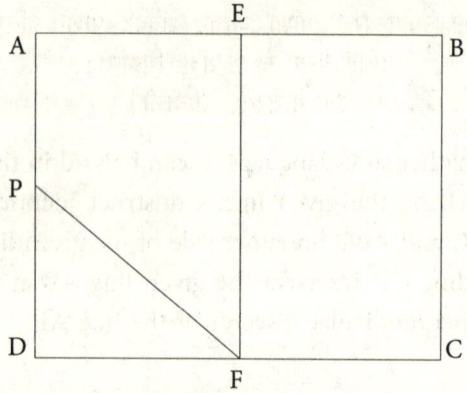

Let a and b be the sides of the two given square such that a>b. Let us assume that ABCD be a square of side a.

Take points E and F on square in such a way that AE = DF = b. Take a point P on side AD such that PF = EF = a. Join PF, then the square with side DP is our required side.

In triangle PDF,
$$PD^2 = PF^2 - DF^2 = a^2 - b^2$$

**To construct a square of area equal to the sum of two given squares:**

ह्रसीयसः करण्या वर्षीयसो वृध्रसुल्लिखेत् ।
वृध्रस्याक्षणायारज्जुरूभे समस्यति ।

The above shloka focuses on how a square of area equal to the sum of two given squares can be constructed. The method is also described in Baudhayana Sulbasutra and Katyayani Sulbasutra as given below.

Let a and b be the sides of the two squares with a > b. Let ABCD be the square with each side = a. Take two points P and Q on AB and DC such that AP = DQ = b. Join AQ.

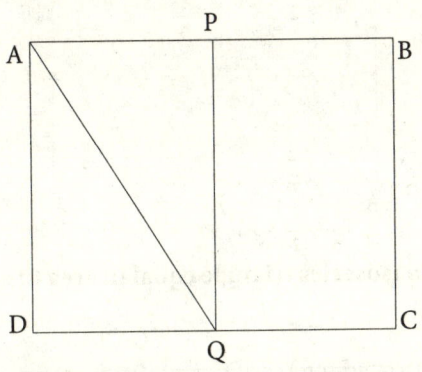

In triangle ADQ,
$$AQ^2 = AD^2 + DQ^2$$
$$= a^2 + b^2$$

## To construct a rhombus of given area:

तावदेव दीर्घचतरश्रं विहृत्य पूर्वापरयोः करण्योर्धात्
तावति दक्षिणोतरयोनिपातयेत् सनित्योभवतः प्रउगम्।

Drawing a rectangle of the same area (i.e. of the area of the square for the prauga), one should draw lines from the middle points of the eastern and western sides to the middles of the southern and northern sides that it the rhombus of the same area.

Let ABCD be a rectangle of twice the area of rhombus. Let E, F, G, H be the middle points of the side AB, BC, CD, and AD. Join EF, FG, GH and HE.

Ar (Rhombus EFGH) = 1/2 ar( Rectangle ABCD)

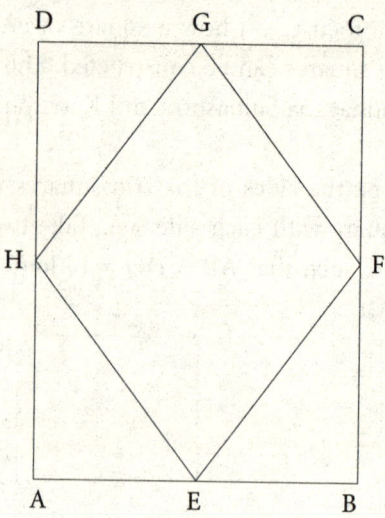

**To construct an isosceles triangle equal in area to a given square and vice versa:**

यावनग्निस्सारन्निप्रादेशो द्विस्तावर्तीं भूमिं चतुरश्र कृत्वा
पूर्वस्याः करण्या अर्धत श्रोणी प्रत्यालिखेत्
स नित्या प्रउगम् ।

Making an area which is double as much as the fire altar with the arantis and pradesas, into a square, one should draw lines from the middle point of the eastern side towards the bottom corners. This is the equivalent prauga (isosceles triangle).

Let ABCD be a square of twice the required area. Let E be the middle point of CD. Join EA and EB, then AEB is the required triangle. If EF is the altitude drawn then the squae id divided into 2 equal rectangles AFED and FBCE.

ar(AFE) = 1/2 rectangle AFED and
ar( FBE) = 1/2 rectangle FBCE
Hence,
ar(AEB) = 1/2 ABCE

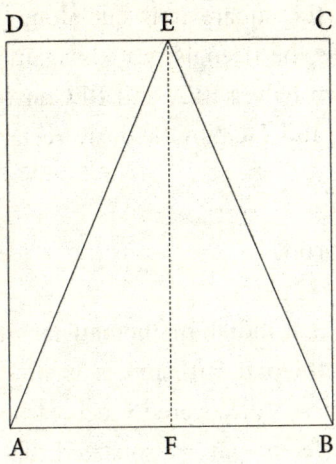

## To construct a rectangle equal to a given square in area:

समचतरश्रं दीर्घचतुरश्रं चिकीर्षन् मध्येऽक्ष्णयापच्छिद्य
विभच्येतरत्पुसस्तादुतारतश्चेपदध्यात् ।
विषमं चेद्यथायोगं उपसंहरेदिति व्यासः ।

Wishing to transform a square into a rectangle one should cut diagonally in the middle, divide one part again and place the two halves to the north and east of the other part. If the figure is a quadrilateral one should place together as it fits. This is the distribution.

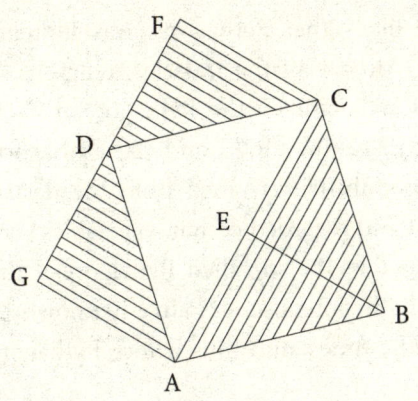

Let ABCD be the square it is cut along AC to form two right angle triangles the triangle ABC is again halved along the altitude BE. The two halves BEA and BEC are then removed to the positions DFC and DGA. Obviously rectangle ACFG and= Square ABCD.

## Pythagoras Theorem

It is a recorded fact that Indian mathematicians were much ahead of the Western mathematicians and it is no surprise that the Pythagoras theorem was discovered much earlier by Indians and Sulbasutra has its reference. It is also stated that Pythagoras who lived around 500 BC visited India and interacted with Indian mathematicians and scholars.

Fracois-Marie Arouet de Voltaire wrote:

'I am convinced that everything has come down to us from the banks of the Ganga- Astronomy, Astrology, Spiritualism, etc. It is very important to note that 2500 years ago at least Pythagoras went from Samos to the Ganga to learn Geometry... But he would certainly not have undertaken such a strange journey had the reputation of the Brahmins' science not been long established in Europe.'

Professor H.G. Rawlinson writes:

'It is more likely that Pythagoras was influenced by India than by Egypt. Almost all the theories, religions, philosophical and mathematical taught by the Pythagoreans, were known in India in the sixth century B.C., and the Pythagoreans, like the Jains and the Buddhists, refrained from the destruction of life and eating meat and regarded certain vegetables such as beans as taboo" "It seems that the so-called Pythagorean theorem of the quadrature of the hypotenuse was already known to the Indians in the older Vedic times, and thus before Pythagoras.'

In Bodhayana Sulbasutra (1.12) there is a reference to Pythagoras Theorem known as bhuja- koti—karna-nyaya which is as follows:

दीर्घचतुरश्रस्य अक्ष्णयारज्जु पार्श्वमानी तिर्यंगमानी
चय त् पृथग्भूते कुरूतः तदुभयं करोति ।

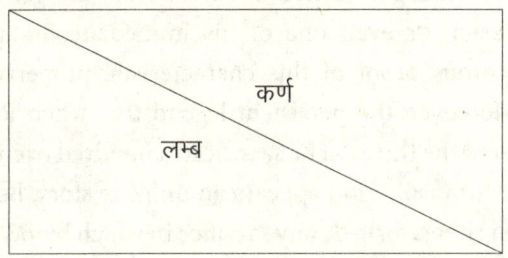

दीर्घचतुरश्रम = (lit. longish 4-sided figure)
अक्ष्णया रज्जुः– the diagonal rope
पार्श्वमानी :– the measure of the lateral side
तिर्यंगमानी :– the measure of the perpendicular side

Baudahayana used a rope as an example in the above shloka which can be translated as: The rope corresponding to the diagonal of a rectangle makes whatever is made by the lateral and the vertical sides individually.

This is clearly the most intuitive way to understand the Pythagoras theorem during that period. The Baudhayana Sulbasutra says that a rope stretched along the length of the diagonal produces an area which the vertical and horizontal sides make together. Baudhayana also states that if a and b be the two sides and c be the hypotenuse such that a is divisible by 4 then c = (a—a/8) + b/2.

There is no evidence that the authors of Sulbasutra proved the so-called Pythagoras theorem. F. Cajoi writes:

'This proof was unknown in Europe till Wallis rediscovered it. The Sulva sutra indicates that the Hindus, perhaps as early as 800 BC, applied geometry in the construction of altars.'

David M. Burton was also of the view that Pythagoras theorem was discovered in India and not by Pythagoras. He writes:

'Because none of the various Greek writers who attributed the theorem to Pythagoras lived within five centuries of him, there is a little convincing evidence to corroborate the general belief that the master, or even one of his immediate disciples, gave the first rigorous proof of this characteristic property of right triangles. Moreover, the persistent legend that when Pythagoras had discovered the theorem he sacrificed a hundred oxen to Muses in gratitude for inspiration appears an unlikely story, because the Pythagorean rituals forbade any sacrifice in which blood was shed.'

Apart from the Baudhayana Sulbasutra, the Katyayana Sulva Sutra also mentions about the Pythagoras Theorem in the following verse:

दीर्घचतुरश्रस्य अक्ष्णयारज्जुः तिर्यगमानी पार्श्वमानी च यत्
पृथग्भूते कुरूतः तदुभयं करोति इति क्षेत्रज्ञानम् ।।

Even the so-called Pythagoras theorem is in Manava Sulbasutra. Look at the following verse of Manava Sulbasutra:

आयामं आयामगुणं विस्तारं विस्तारेण तु।
समस्य वर्गमूलंय त् तत् कर्ण तद्विदो विदुः।।

Using the modern notation, the verse can be mathematically translated as:

$$\sqrt{\text{आयाम}^2 + \text{विस्तार}^2} = \text{कर्ण}$$

T. K. Puttaswamy in his book *Mathematical Achievements of Pre-modern Indian Mathematicians* clearly mentions that the author of Sulbasutra had the knowledge of triplets and so while performing yagnas and making altars thereof the size of Yagna Kunda followed the Pythagorean triplets. The following right triangles have been mentioned in the Sulbasutra.

| Perpendicular | Base | Hypotenuse | Author of Sulbasutra |
|---|---|---|---|
| 3 | 4 | 5 | Apasthamba / Baudhayana |
| 5 | 12 | 13 | Apasthamba / Baudhayana |
| 7 | 24 | 25 | Apasthamba / Baudhayana |
| 12 | 35 | 37 | Apasthamba / Baudhayana |
| 15 | 36 | 39 | Apasthamba / Baudhayana |
| 2½ | 6 | 6½ | Manava |
| 7½ | 10 | 12½ | Manava |
| 40 | 96 | 104 | Manava |
| 72 | 96 | 120 | Manava |

तासां त्रिकचतुष्कयोः, द्वादशिकपंञ्चिकयोः
पंचदशिकाष्टिकयोः, सप्तिकचतुर्विंशकयोः
द्वादशिरकपंचत्रिंशिकयोः, पंचदशिकष्टत्रिंशिकयोः
इत्येतासु उपलब्धिः।

The Soutramani altar were constructed with sides 5√3, 12√3, 13√3 whereas the Aswa Medha altar was constructed with the sides 15√2, 36√2, 39√2.

## Similar Triangle

B.B. Dutta writes that the properties of similar triangles and parallel lines were known to the ancient Hindus.

At the centre of Jambudvipa there is known to be mountain Mandara by name whose height above the earth is 99000 yojanas, whose depth below is 1000 yojanas; its diameter at the base is 1090 10/11 yojanas at the ground 10000 yojanas. Then its diameter diminishes by degrees until at the top it is 1000 yojanas. Its circumference at the base is 31910 5/11 yojanas, at the ground 31623 yojanas and the top a little over 3162 yojanas. It is broader at the base, contracted at the middle and still shorter at the top and is of the form of a cow's tail (a truncated right cone).

To find the diameter of any other section parallel to the base Jinabhadra Gani gives the following rule:

Wherever is wanted the diameter of (the Mandara), the descent from the top of the Mandara divided by 11 and then added to a 1000 will give the diameter. The ascent from the bottom should be similarly divided by 11 and the quotient subtracted from the diameter of the base. What remains will be the diameter there (i.e., at that height) of that (Mandara).

## Square Root of 2

Baudhayana Sulbasutra gives the approximate value of √2 up to 4 decimal places correctly.

समस्य दिकरणी। प्रमाणं तृतीयेन वर्धयेत्,<br>तच्चतुर्थेनात्म चतुस्त्रिंशोनेन सविशेषतः।

In simple words,

$$\sqrt{2} \approx 1 + \frac{1}{3} + \frac{1}{3.4} - \frac{1}{3.4.34} = \frac{577}{408} \approx 1.414216,$$

## Squaring a Circle

Squaring a circle remain the problem of antiquity for centuries. This problem is of great importance in connection with the Vedic sacrifices. The three sacrifice altars—Grahapatya, Ahavaniva and Daksina—were of the same area/size, but of different in shapes—square, circular and semi-circular. The three shapes mentioned in Taittriya Samhita (3000 BC)—Rathacakra-citi, Samuhya-citi, and Paricayya-citi—one had to draw in each case a square equal to that of Syena-citi and then to transform it into a circle. To construct a square whose area is equal to that of a given circle better known as squaring a circle and that too with the help of a scale and compass was a tough job to accomplish. But it is a matter of pride for Indians as this very problem and vice versa was solved by the authors of Sulbasutra. Interestingly this problem also helped the rishis of Sulbasutra to find the approximate value of pi ($\pi$) much before the Biblical value of pi = 3 discussed in the first chapter itself.

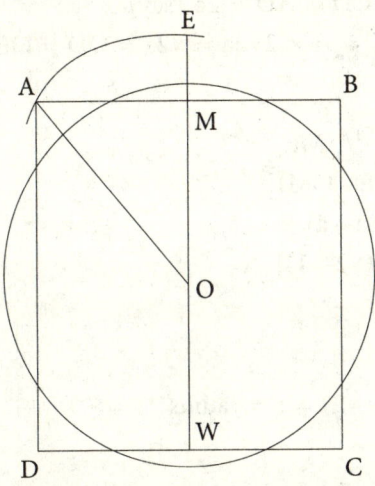

Baudhayana gave a very interesting construction for a circle whose area is equal to that of a given square. Baudhayana says:

चतुरश्रं मण्डलं चिकीर्षन् अक्ष्णयार्धं मध्यात् प्राचीम्
अभ्यापातयेत्य दादतिशिष्यते तस्य सह तृतीयेन मण्डलं परिलिखेत्।

If you wish to circle a square, draw half of its diagonal about the centre towards the east west line; then describe a circle together with a third part of that which lies outside the square.

## Proof

Let ABCD be a square which is to be transformed into a circle so that their area is the same. Let O be the central point of the square. Join OA. Now with O as centre and OA as radius draw a circle intersecting the East-West line at E. Divide EM at P such that EP = 2 PM, where M is the midpoint of the side AB. With O as centre and OP as radius draw a circle. The area of this circle is roughly equal in area to that of the square ABCD.

$$AB = BC = CD = AD = 2a \text{ (say)}$$
$$OA = \tfrac{1}{2} AC = \tfrac{1}{2} \times 2\sqrt{2}a = \sqrt{2}a = OD = OE$$

Therefore,

$$OP = OM + \tfrac{1}{3} ME$$
$$= a + \tfrac{1}{3} (OE-OM)$$
$$= a + \tfrac{1}{3} (\sqrt{2}a-a)$$
$$= a [1 + \tfrac{1}{3} (\sqrt{2}-1)]$$
$$= \tfrac{a}{3} (2 +\sqrt{2})$$

Hence,

$$OP = \tfrac{a}{3} (2 +\sqrt{2}) = r = \text{radius}$$

Therefore,

$$a = \frac{3\,r}{(2 +\sqrt{2})}$$

$$4a^2 = \frac{4\times 9\,r^2}{(2 +\sqrt{2})^2} = \text{(Area of Square)}$$

$$= \frac{36 \times r^2}{(2 +\sqrt{2})^2}$$

We know that
Area of circle = $\pi r^2$
Hence,

$$\pi = \frac{36}{(2 + \sqrt{2})}$$

$$= \frac{36 \times (2 - \sqrt{2})^2}{(2 + \sqrt{2})^2 \times (2 - \sqrt{2})^2}$$

$$= \frac{36 \times (4 + 2 - 4\sqrt{2})^2}{4}$$

$$= 9 \, (6 - 4\sqrt{2}) = 3.088$$

## Sri Yantra

The geometrical knowledge of Indian mathematics reached its peak when they constructed the Sri Yantra, consisting of nine interwoven isosceles triangle that involves a quality work and sound knowledge of geometry.

The Sri Yantra a sacred symbol in Hindu religion has its origin in the Atharva Veda. The oldest Sri Yantra is appeared in the Sringeri Matha established by the famous philosopher Adi Shankaracharya in the eighth century. As far as mathematics in Sri Yantra is concerned, I myself was amazed to see the geometrical interference of Sri Yantra with high class of geometry used at that time with precision is an extraordinary work done during Vedicera.

The Sri Yantra is a diagram formed by 9 interlocking triangles that surround and radiate out from the central point. It consists of a central 14 angles sealed with 8 and 16 petalled lotus. The interlocking 9 triangles produces 43 small triangles. The bindu at the centre of it represents Goddess Tripura Sundari. The Goddess defines the beauty of three worlds भू (Earth), भूवः (Atmosphere), स्वः(Sky). The nine isosceles triangles of Sri Yantra has two sections. The four isosceles triangles with the vertex upwards represents Lord Shiva and his masculine powers; the five downwards isosceles triangles represents the female power of Goddess Durga or Shakti.

Thus the Sri yantra is the combination of masculine and feminine power of god. The 9 triangles form 43 smaller triangles in such a way that it symbolize the entire cosmos or a womb symbolic of creation. This is surrounded by a lotus of 8 petals and 16 petals and an earth square resembling a temple with four doors. The meaning of each smaller triangles and square is defined as:

1. *Trailokya Mohan* or *Bhupar*, a square of three lines with four portals
2. *Sarva Aasa Paripurak*, a sixteen-petal lotus
3. *Sarva Sankshobahan*, an eight-petal lotus
4. *Sarva Saubhagyadayak*, composed of fourteen small triangles
5. *Sara Arthasadhak*, composed of ten small triangles
6. *Sarva Rakshakar*, composed of ten small triangles
7. *Sarva Rogahar*, composed of eight small triangles
8. *Sarva Siddhiprada*, composed of 1 small triangle
9. *Sarva Anandamay*, composed of a point or *bindu*

*Sri Yantra with 43 triangles*
*(Source : Wikipedia)*

Shankaracharya in *Saundrya Lahiri* says: 'By reason of the four Srikanthas (Srikantha is an epithet of Siva) and the five damsels of Siva (which have the nature of Sakti), which are penetrated by Sambhu (i.e., bindu—the dot in the centre) and constitute the nine fundamental natures. The 43 angles of your dwelling place are evolved, along with the 8-petalled and 16-petalled lotuses, the circles and the three lines.'

It is an astonishing fact that a very large, perfectly formed Sri Yantra was discovered into the dry lake bed in Oregon, near the Idaho boarder by an Air National Guard pilot in 1990. This symbol was over a quarter of mile in length, and consisted of over 13 miles of lines etched into the impacted mud 3"–10" deep.

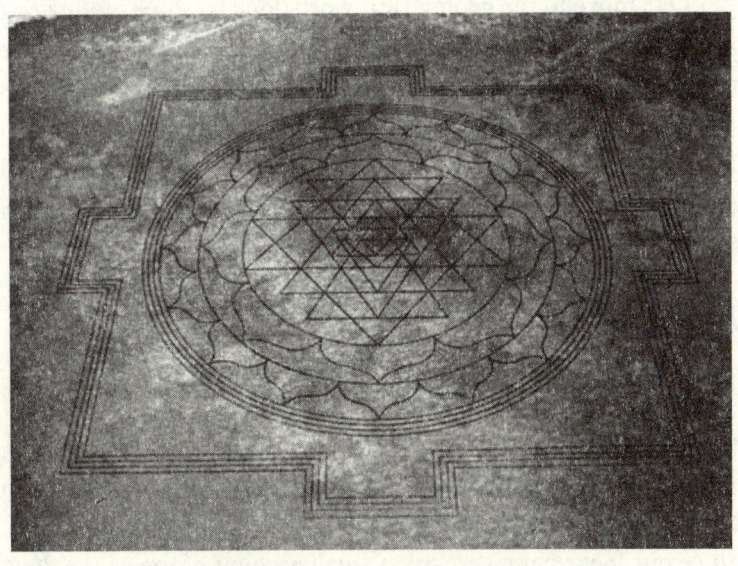

*Sri Yantra found in Oregon lake*
*(Copyright of this image lies with Bill Witherspoon)*

The important geometrical aspect of this yantra is that the triangles are arranged in such a way that they produce 43 subsidiary triangles with a big dot called the bindu at the centre of the smallest triangle. The construction of the diagram with perfection is really a challenge as all the intersections should be correct and the vertices of the largest triangles fall on the circumference of the enclosing circles. In all cases the base angles of the largest triangles is about 51.5°.

This clearly shows that the rishis of Vedic era could construct triangles, equilateral and isosceles; quadrilaterals, square, rectangle, rhombus, trapezium; and also the circle. They could also find the area of all these mathematical figures by their own sutras. The fact that they knew the Pythagoras Theorem, triplets, the value of pi and square root of 2 and 3 shows the brilliance of their mathematical expertise.

Let's move to the geometrical work done by some of the great mathematicians of India. The important point which I would like to make here is that I have put down only the important results related to geometry. There might be some other result which I haven't mentioned here due to paucity of time and I would request the readers to research more on the subject if they wish to learn further.

## Aryabhata

The great Aryabhata was born in 476 AD and has done a lot of work in algebra, geometry and trigonometry. In the first chapter, I have discussed that Aryabhata was the first mathematician to have given the approximate value of pi up to 4 decimal places. Since our focus here is to give a small account of the works done by him I shall only discuss the results not its proof in detail. Here are some of the great works of Aryabhata:

- He was the first to give the formula to find the area of a triangle.

त्रिभुजस्य फलशरीरं समदलकोटी भुजार्धसंवर्गः ।
ऊर्ध्व भुजा तत्संवर्गाधि स धनः षडश्रिरिति ।।

The product of the perpendicular (from the vertex to the base) and half the base give the measure of the area of a triangle.

Hence,

Area of triangle = 1/2 × base × perpendicular from the vertex

- He has postulated a theorem relating to circle, 'In a circle the product of two Sara is the square of the half cord of the two arcs, i.e., a × b = $c^2$, where c is half the chord and the saras or arrows are the segments of a diameter which bisect any chord.'
- Aryabhata has defined the area of a trapezium to be the product of half the sum of the parallel sides and the altitude. In the following shloka he has also given the formula to find the area of circle and volume of sphere.

समपरिणाहस्यार्ध विष्कं भार्धहतमेव वृतफलम् ।
तन्निजमूलेन हतं घन गोल फलं निखशेषम ।।

Which means,

Area of trapezium = 1/2 × (sum of parallel sides) × altitude

## Brahmagupta

This Indian mathematician was born in 598 AD. He was a resident of Bhinamala, situated on the northern border of Gujarat. At the age of 30, he had composed his great work Brahma Sphuta Siddhanta that contains 24 chapters and 1008 verses. Here are his contribution to geometry.

1. The Pythagoras theorem was known much earlier and had been mentioned in Sulbasutra but Brahmagupta concentrated on right-angled triangles and quadrilateral

and done some modification and gave a general solution for a rational right-angled triangle with sides 2mn, $m^2 - n^2$ and $m^2 + n^2$.

2. He was the first mathematician to give the formula to find an area of cyclic quadrilateral with sides a, b, c and d. According to Brahmagupta:

भुजयोगार्धचतुष्टय भुजोनघातात् पदं सूक्ष्मम्

The exact area of a cyclic quadrilateral is the square root of the product of four sets of half the sum of the sides diminished by the sides. Area of cyclic quadrilateral = $\{s\,(s-a)\,(s-b)\,(s-c)\,(s-d)\}^{1/2}$; where $2s = a + b + c + d$

3. Brahmagupta has also given the rule to find the length of diagonals of a cyclic quadrilateral whose sides are a, b, c and d.

कर्णाश्रित भुज घातैक्यमुभयथा ऽन्यो ऽन्यत्र भाजितं गुणयेत ।
योगेन भुज प्रतिभुज वधयोः कर्णो पदे विषमे ।।

If x and y are the diagonal of cyclic quadrilateral then

$$x = \sqrt{\frac{(ad + bc)\,(ac + bd)}{(ad + bc)}}$$

$$y = \sqrt{\frac{(ab + cd)\,(ac + bd)}{(ad + bc)}}$$

Brahmagupta also gave a rule for the volume of frustum of a pyramid with squares of sides' $s_1$ and $s_2$; substantially as:

Volume = $h/3\,(s_1^2 + s_2^2 + s_1 \times s_2)$

Bhaskaracharya and Mahavira have also given some formulas to find the area and volume of circle, volume of sphere, area of sphere and many more. It is worth mentioning here that for obtaining the circum-radius of a cyclic quadrilateral in terms of the sides, Paamesvara (1360–1455) was probably the first to give a formula in his commentary in *Lilavati*.

'The three sums of the products of the sides, taken two at a time, are to be multiplied together and divided by the product of the sums of the sides taken three at a time and diminished by the fourth. If a circle is drawn with the square root of this quantity as radius the whole quadrilateral will be situated in it.'

Hence, if a, b, c and d are the sides of the cyclic quadrilateral and r its circum-radius then:

$$r = \frac{(ab + cd)\ (ac + bd)\ (ad + bc)}{(a + b + c - d)\ (b + c + d - a)\ (d + a + b - c)}$$

The advancement in modern geometry would not have been possible had the Indians rishis not started the process of constructing altars for worshiping gods. The beauty of the ancient geometry can be seen in the precision of making altars without any scale and compass. The construction of isosceles triangles in Sri Yantra, the concept of falcon-shaped altar and the construction of mahavedi in shape of a trapezium are all done without the use of any advanced technology of computer, tape and scale.

# BIBLIOGRAPHY

Dwivedi, Kapildev. *The Prosody of Pingala*. Vishwavidyalaya Prakshan.

Hooda, D.S. *Aryabhata* 2008.

Iyengar, T.R.R. *Hinduism and Scientific Quest*. Zen Publication 2004.

Knapp, Stephen. *A Complete Review of Vedic Literature and the Knowledge Within*, 2012.

Naegele, Charles J. *Ancient History of India: Manusmriti Revisitied*. 2011.

'National Programme on Technology Enhanced Learning.' 'NPTEL course on Mathematics in India: From Vedic Period to Modern Times.' Available online at nptel.ac.in/courses/111101080/.

Patwardhan, Krishnaji Shankara. 2014. *Lilavati of Bhaskaracharya*. Motilal Banarshi Das Publication.

Priyadarshi, P. *India's Contribution to the West*. Standard Publishers. 2004.

Rao, S. Balachandra. *Indian Mathematics and Astronomy*. Jnana Deep Publications.

Thaibaut, George. *The Sulvasutras*. D.K. Publishers.

सूर्य सिद्धांत–प्रो. रामचंद्रपांडे–चौखंभा प्रकाशन

गणित शास्त्र के विकास में भारतीय परंपरा–डा. सुद्युम्न आचार्य–मोतीलाल बनारसीदास

प्राचीन सभ्यताओ में विज्ञान एवं तकनीक–डा0 रजनीकांत पंत

प्राचीन भारत में गणित–रत्न कुमार ठाकुर–छत्तीसगढ़ राज्य हिंदी ग्रंथ अकादमी

रामायण–गीता प्रेस गोरखपुर

## Research Articles

Bag, A.K. 1990. 'Ritual Geometry in India and its Parallelism in other Cultural Areas', *Indian Journal of History of Sciences*, 25(1-4).

Dutta, Amartya Kumar. 2012. 'Mathematics in Ancient India'. *Resonance.*

Gupta, R.C. 2003. 'Agni-Kundas—A Neglected Area of Study in the History of Ancient Indian Mathematics', *Indian Journal of History of Science*, 38(1), pp. 1-15.

Gurudeo Anand Tularam. 2010. 'Vedas and the Development of Arithmetic and Algebra', *Journal of Mathematics and Statistics* 6(4) : 468-480.

Kak, Subhash C. 1993. 'Astronomy of the Satapatha Brahmana', *Indian Journal of History of Science* 28(1).

Krishnaswami Ayyangar, A.A. 'Peeps into India's Mathematical Past'. Electronic Journal of Vedic Studies (EJVS), Vol. 10 (2003), Issue 6 (Nov. 14) pp. 1-18. (©) ISSN 1084-7561.

Murthy, S.S. 'Number Symbolism in the Vedas'. Electronic Journal of Vedic Studies (EJVS), Vol. 10 (2003), Issue 6 (Nov. 14) pp. 1-18. (©) ISSN 1084-7561.

———'A note on the Ramayana'. Electronic Journal of Vedic Studies (EJVS), Vol. 10 (2003), Issue 6 (Nov. 14) pp. 1-18. (©) ISSN 1084-7561.

Pavlovich Kulaichev, Alexey. 1984. 'Sriyantra and Its Mathematical Properties', *Indian Journal of History of Sciences*, 19(3): 279-292.

Sivanandan, D.S. 'The Continuity of Sulbasutra Traditional as Evident in the Agnichayana Rituals of Kerala—A Critical Study'.

## Websites

- MacTutor Archive
- www.hindupedia.com
- www.wikipedia.com
- www.robinstewart.com